A Grave Misunderstanding

A Simon Grave Mystery

Len Boswell

BLACK ROSE
writing™

D1478672

The final approval for this literary material is granted by the author.

Second printing

This is a work of fiction. Names, characters, businesses, places, events and incidents are either the products of the author's imagination or used in a fictitious manner. Any resemblance to actual persons, living or dead, or actual events is purely coincidental.

ISBN: 978-1-61296-900-8   .
PUBLISHED BY BLACK ROSE WRITING
www.blackrosewriting.com

Printed in the United States of America
Suggested Retail Price (SRP) $18.95

A Grave Misunderstanding is printed in Palatino Linotype

To all I love without condition,
To all I love without omission.
Never doubt.

Jen Boswell

A Grave Misunderstanding

"Logic: The art of thinking and reasoning in strict accordance with the limitations and incapacities of the human misunderstanding."
—Ambrose Bierce

"It may be added, to prevent misunderstanding, that when I speak of contemplated objects . . . as objects of contemplation, the act of contemplation itself is of course an enjoyment."
—Samuel Alexander

"There's never going to be a great misunderstanding of me. I think I'm a little whacked."
—Pamela Anderson

1

Her naked body was displayed just so, arms and legs splayed like a paper doll, head gently resting on the bottom step as if she had slid down the staircase on her back, blond hair carefully fanned out to form a waterfall to the foyer floor, a single red rose placed between her teeth in a way that suggested flamenco dancing, a child's suction-cup arrow sticking out from her forehead, and most disturbing, an emoji painted on her belly with red paint, its eyes crosses, indicating death, its mouth the poor woman's belly button, giving the emoji a look of both surprise and dismay. All this gave Detective Simon Grave the distinct feeling that lunch would be delayed.

Simon Grave had been a detective in Crab Cove for more than twenty years, and in all those years, he had never once had a case involving a murder in a mansion. So as thrilling as it was to see a body sprawled on a staircase with more steps than the Washington Monument, under a chandelier capable of lighting Dubuque, Iowa, he had grave misgivings that the CSI folks, a crew capable of almost nothing, would be up to the task at hand.

As for hands, he couldn't help but notice that the victim had only one, at least within her reach. The severed hand lay several feet away, looking gray and bloodless, like a dead fish washed ashore on a beach in Detective Grave's price range. Jeremy Polk, the medical examiner, was poking at it with a Q-tip and making little headway in reanimating it.

"I say, Polk, what do you make of all this?"

Polk stopped poking the hand and looked up at Grave. "You

mean the body or those annoying people knocking on the door of the locked room upstairs?"

"The body, of course." He wasn't ready to discuss the locked room and the people within, despite the rapidity and forcefulness of their knocking, not to mention the strident though muffled obscenities they were yelling and screaming through the door, which his trained ear noticed was reverberating within the tonal range of aged mahogany.

The fact was, he had only dealt with murders where the locked room contained the victim, not what may be all the prime suspects.

Polk set down the Q-tip and groaned his way to his feet, drawing his body to its full height, which wasn't much. He was an altogether short man by any measure, but there was something about his posture—back rigid, chest thrust out, head tilted to one side, chin up, nose high, lips curled into an arch snarl, one brow higher than the other—that suggested he might be almost an inch taller and certainly a man to be reckoned with, if not taken seriously, particularly on a weekend. In short, if "height" was a hot air balloon soaring above the desert, Polk was a small cactus staring up at it.

"You can see the body right there, Grave."

"Yes, of course, but what do you make of all these clues?"

"Clues?" said Polk, shaking his head dismissively. "In case you haven't noticed, it's all about DNA these days. All we have to do is take DNA kits upstairs, collect samples from the likely suspects, match their DNA to the evidence from and around this unfortunate young woman, and we'll have our killer. Ipso facto, e pluribus unum."

The medical examiner had then laughed in a way that gave Detective Grave pause. He was unsure about the nature of the laugh. On the one hand, it was pure sardonic mischief, while on the other hand it had all the qualities of a dismissive chuckle. He could have gone on to third and fourth hands, but he preferred to be anatomically correct in such matters.

"Polk, I fully recognize the relentless intrusion of science on criminal detection, but remember, DNA spelled backwards is "AND." There's always something else, there's always an "and," whether it's a careless remark or something as simple as a poorly timed laugh, there's always something else to hoist the criminal on his own petard."

Polk rolled his eyes and laughed a second time. "Well, say what you will, Grave, but I'd rather bring DNA evidence to court than a poorly timed laugh."

This second laugh was clearly dismissive, coming as it did with eyes that seemed to roll hard, like dice thrown down a craps table by a man down to his last toss, set to lose everything, including the blonde on his arm.

Grave tried his best to shake off the troubling image. Polk with a beautiful blonde? Ridiculous. He decided to move on.

"Is there anyone else around?"

"Just me and the usual carnival of uniforms," said Polk, sweeping his arms around the room to take in what must have been a dozen uniformed officers, each trying their best to look busy, but most just gawking at the interior of the mansion and looking forward to describing it to their wives or girlfriends.

"No, I mean, if *everyone's* locked in that room upstairs, who called this in?"

Polk couldn't believe his ears. "What? Have you never heard of cellphones?"

Grave hated to be caught in a logical mistake, particularly by a man like Polk. "Er, yes, of course."

Polk laughed again in a way that might be classified a curt guffaw, coming out as it did like the bark of a small dog. "Well, as it turns out, there was no emergency call, at least from the crazy stupid people upstairs. Turns out, the lord of the manor here didn't turn up for his tee time at the country club, which some of his golfing buddies considered tantamount to murder. One thing led to another, a patrol car was dispatched, etcetera, etcetera, and here we are with a beautiful dead woman on a Saturday morning. Oh, and shortly after we arrived, we received an email from someone upstairs."

"I see," said Grave. "I'll leave you to your precious DNA, then." He turned on his heels and started climbing the stairs, which seemed to lead endlessly upward to some insanely artistic vanishing point.

Polk laughed yet again behind him. "You can't accept the primacy of DNA, can you?"

"I can't, shan't, wan't," he said, continuing to proceed up the stairs without looking back.

"You know," said Polk, "that *wan't* isn't a word."

Grave paused on the stairway and looked back at Polk. "How would you know without checking its DNA? And besides, it rhymes."

He continued walking up the stairs, the silence from Polk nearly unbearable. He made a mental note to brush up on his skills in rational argument, at least where contractions were concerned.

After a few more steps, he paused again to give his throbbing legs a rest and to look back on the crime scene. Even at 30,000 feet, the approximate height of the mansion's staircase, a crime scene could reveal important clues. In Grave's experience, murder was often the result of a misunderstanding, of fact, situation, or intent. And the more grave the misunderstanding, the more chaotic the crime scene, indicating a level of passion, whether from hate or love, disproportionate to the perceived slight. But the crime scene he was looking at here, even from this rarified altitude, was not chaotic at all. In fact, it was clearly a planned, and laughably overwrought, tableau.

The pounding coming from upstairs continued unabated. He climbed on, his stomach rumbling from hunger.

2

The stairs seemed to go on and on, testing his fitness, his calves and thighs burning from the effort until he finally reached the landing of the second floor, revealing hallways left and right that seemed to outdo the stairway in length, each stretching on forever, with doors every twenty feet or so, indicating enough bedrooms to house every member of Congress, not that bedrooms and Congressmen was ever a good idea. The carpeting on the floor, which must have been a wonderful golden color in days past, was well worn and smelled of dust and mildew. Things were not as mansion fresh as he would have expected given the pristine wonder of the marble staircase.

Polk called out to him from below.

"You're not really going to go in there dressed like that, are you? You look like a damned Italian gigolo."

He waved him off and returned his attention to the door in front of him, which was indeed mahogany, aged to near black and thrumming from the sound of pounding fists.

He was clearly no Italian gigolo, although he could claim Italian heritage through his mother, Maria, who provided wildly gesticulated counterpoint to his father, a reticent man of German descent, who could be found, even today, sitting on a plastic-encased recliner and crinkling his way through sitcom after sitcom, their laugh tracks the ribald soul of his existence.

On the other hand, Grave was certainly dressed for the part: powder blue boating shoes and a matching blue shirt above crisp, white linen slacks, a yellow sweater draped across his shoulders and tied causally into a knot in front to suggest that he was out for the day, perhaps for the entire evening if he could find just the right companion.

In truth, he had planned to spend the day in an outdoor café near the marina, sipping at a latte and hoping to attract a beautiful woman, his clothing a bright deception, like a fishing lure, suggesting that one of the yachts bobbing in the harbor was his and that he was a prime morsel of vintage manliness for any woman who might happen by with yachthood in mind.

Not that he really needed such deceptions. He was one of those men that people described as lean, a pleasant midway point between skinny and grotesquely muscular, the kind of man that suggested dalliance, if not outright debauchery, both of which were far from the core of Grave's personality, which tended more toward Dudley Do-Right with a soupçon of a slightly off, less deductive Sherlock Holmes thrown in.

He was tall, but not basketball tall, and square-jawed to be sure, and held his chin skyward, suggesting both arrogance and innate innocence, or at least a long attention span. His eyes were blue in the way that ice calved from a glacier is blue, and gray in a way that clouds were gray before a storm, hovering betwixt the two on most days, but definitely tending toward storm clouds when he was on a case, their turbulence causing many a suspect to avoid eye contact and want to drop to his knees in confession.

His nose was strong and prominent, with a little speed bump in the middle, the result of a wicked left cross from the fists of his childhood friend Ray Pickins, who like most of his friends, had disappeared into the mists of time.

He had lips, of course, and they moved more or less as lips should do when he talked, but there was not much to say about them. His hair was something else entirely: thick and black and glistening from the combined effects of shampoos and conditioners faithfully applied each morning and topped with just enough gel to hold each wavelet in place.

Not that there weren't chinks in his armor of good looks. He had just turned forty-two, an event that now had him either avoiding mirrors entirely or standing in front of them for long periods pushing at his skin, which was rapidly losing its elasticity and seemed to be on a death march to aged parchment. Women were not looking at him with the same level of lust, which is why he had chosen Italian gigolo as his clothing motif this morning instead of his usual gray suit. In short, if "handsome" was a basketball team, he would have been the player the coach sent in during the last three seconds of the game, when the team was either thirty points ahead or thirty points behind, and his presence on the court would have little effect on the outcome. He was handsome, but just.

Without turning around, he shouted down to Polk. "Send Sergeant Blunt up with the DNA kits when he arrives, will you?"

No response.

He shrugged, ran a hand through his hair, took one step forward, and unlocked the door with a twist of the knob on the deadbolt, the mahogany cacophony stopping abruptly as he pushed the door open to slowly reveal the bright panorama of the room and the aggravated people within.

3

The first thing he noticed upon opening the door was the arrow heading straight for his head, which he plucked from the air an inch from his nose, its suction cup dripping with the spit of the small boy across the room in full Native American costume, including the full-feathered headdress of a war chief.

The mouths of the six other people in the room gasped, some from horror at the actions of the boy, some from regret that the arrow had missed its mark, and some clearly from admiration of his skills and reflexes, which were self-described as "catlike" on the brief biography he had posted on the precinct's website.

In truth, the room was smaller than he had expected, no more than a brightly lit and cramped artist's studio, paintings—all of red fish—in various stages of completion stacked against and covering every wall, a large easel at the room's center, the artist herself standing behind it, head stuck out peering at him with what looked like lustful interest, her brush dripping red paint, which seemed to be the only color on her palette.

The back wall of the studio was all windows, floor to ceiling, making it the perfect room for an artist, but not necessarily a detective, the sun making silhouettes of everyone in the room. He held a hand up to partially block the light, revealing a total of seven suspects: the young Indian chief, the *artiste en rose*, an older man, an older woman, a young woman in a nurse's uniform, another youngish woman in a wheelchair, obviously the twin of the artist, and a tall gentleman in a tuxedo who could only be the butler, so stiff was his posture and deferent his attitude as he stood next to the fortyish couple.

He closed the door behind him and took another step into the room, trying his best to establish his authority, or what authority he could muster dressed as he was like an Italian gigolo.

The older man in the turtleneck, perhaps in his late forties, took a tentative step toward him. "Are you Reginald from the marina? I'm afraid I sold the yacht yesterday, and—"

"No, sir," Grave said, flashing his badge. "I am Detective Simon Grave, and I think you know why I am here."

The man looked mystified and confused. "But how—how—could you know about this already?"

"We'll get to that, I'm sure, but for now, who are you and the others, and how did you come to be locked in this room?"

The man gathered himself and scanned the room as if he was unaware of exactly who was in the room and needed to do a head count. "I am Darius Hawthorne. You may know me as the fabulously wealthy CEO of Ramrod Robotics, makers of fine domestic robots. This is my wife, Philomena, my daughter Whitney behind the easel, her twin sister, Edwina, in the wheelchair, our nurse and governess Lola LaFarge next to her, and of course, young Roy Lynn Waters, Whitney's young son, who unfortunately is going through his Indian chief phase."

Grave made notes of all this in his little black book, nodding as each person was identified, and giving each his patented smile of recognition. The wife, fortyish and dressed all in black, looked like an aging Goth. The red-headed artist, thirtyish, was beautiful, if a little crazed looking. Her twin just sat there, beautiful even in a buzz cut, and blankly expressionless, as if she were somewhere else. The nurse was a petite knockout, but seemed to have an attitude; she looked like trouble. The artist's son, maybe eight, looked like he'd had his way more often than not, giving Grave a practiced sneer. That left one more person.

"And the tall gentleman standing next to you?" asked Grave.

Hawthorne laughed, but it was more like a mechanical chuckle, the kind of annoying laugh you might hear coming from behind you in a movie theater, from a person you'd like to punch. "Uncanny, isn't it? He completely fooled you, I see. That's the thing about Ramrod robots—they're so humanlike, so real."

"He's a robot?"

"Well, technically, an android, and more specifically, a Ramrod Robotics Simdroid 3000, Series 2, but yes, a *robot*, if you will. We call him Smithers. It just seems to suit him, particularly since he's been programmed to serve as a butler."

"After the Smithers character in *The Simpsons*?"

Hawthorne shook his head. "Um, no, as obeisant as that character may be, he is not a butler. No, Smithers here is named after Veronica Lodge's butler in the *Archie* comics series.

"Oh, of course." The reference brought back memories of many a college debate over the choice between Betty and Veronica, Grave as indecisive as Archie in the matter. He looked at the robot for some time, trying to find something not human about him, and failed. He turned back to the topic at hand.

"So, how is it that all you fine people—and one robot—came to be locked in this room? And for that matter, why does the room have a door that can only be locked from the outside?"

At this point, Philomena Hawthorne stepped forward.

"The door has been that way since I was a child," she said. "The room was used to house my younger brother, at least for a while. You may remember him as the Dockside Ripper."

Grave blanched. The Dockside Ripper was the most famous serial killer in the history of serial killers, with eighty-seven known kills. His name was Chester Clink, and he was still at large.

"So, your maiden name is Philomena *Clink?*"

"Yes, of the Crab Cove Clinks." She looked down at the old carpeting. "Although we have seen better days."

Grave's head was spinning with the possibilities, including a quick resolution to the murder, but one thing nagged at him—the victim wasn't ripped and stabbed twenty-one times with a Bowie knife. In fact, other than the severed hand, Polk had seen no signs of trauma.

"I'll make a note of that," he said. "So, how did you come to be locked in this room?"

Whitney, the artist, a ravishing redhead with flashing green eyes, stepped from behind the easel. "I can answer that, detective."

Her words did not register in the way that words should usually register, passing through the ears and into the brain, the brain in turn recognizing them, parsing out their meaning from its internal dictionary and book of basic grammar, and then sending signals, including an appropriate verbal response, to the voice box, tongue, and lips.

Her words, in fact, seemed to fall apart and fly around the room as he tried his best to come to grips with the fact that she was completely naked, the brain locking in on the words *curvaceous*, *wondrous*, and *ample*, with a drool response thrown in for good measure. Another word then came to mind: *discombobulated*.

"Why, detective," she said, "what a wonderful shade of red in those manly cheeks of yours. I must capture it for my next painting."

Grave puffed out his cheeks and gave his head a little clearing shake, and tried his best to reply in a way that suggested he was part of the species Homo sapiens sapiens. "Sorry, you startled me."

"Indeed," she said, coyly. "So, to the facts. Everyone, all of us, assembled here last night at exactly eight-*ish* to view my latest work, a painting of the renowned MacGuffin Trophy."

She paused and let the words hang in the air for effect, but seeing none in the face of Detective Grave, she let the words drop to the floor and scurry away before attempting to clarify the situation.

"Surely you've heard of it? The most prized yachting trophy in the world, at least at our local marina, the winning of which sets a skipper apart from all others. And daddy's won it seven times."

Grave shrugged and shook his head.

"Well, that's why you're here, of course," said Hawthorne.

"What?" Grave really was confused.

"The trophy, man, the MacGuffin Trophy!" said Hawthorne.

"It's gone missing," said Whitney with a coquettish shrug of one shoulder.

At this point, Grave was certain he heard the kind of sharply rising chords that an organ would make when a silent movie reached a dramatic turn of events.

But it was just a knock at the door, a tap-tap-tapping and nothing more.

4

Grave motioned everyone to stay in place, went to the door, and opened it. At first he saw nothing, but then a face began to appear, which he eventually recognized as Sergeant Barry Blunt.

"I'll be with you in a moment," Grave whispered. He shut the door before Blunt could reply, and turned back to the people in the room.

"Sergeant Blunt has arrived. I'll let him in the room in just a second, but first I want to explain how we're going to proceed."

The suspects peered back at him blankly.

"First, is there a room nearby where I can meet with each of you privately?"

Philomena looked left and right to see if anyone else would speak up first, then spoke up herself. "There's the library, two doors down on the left. It has a desk and several chairs, and we can bring in tea, coffee, and little crust-free sandwiches if you like. Assuming, of course, you'll let Smithers carry on with his duties."

"Of course," said Grave, motioning to Smithers, who made a slight whirring sound and minced electromechanically to the door and then out of the room.

"Now, Sergeant Blunt will keep you company as I take each of you, one by one, to the library for questioning. I ask that you not talk amongst yourselves during this process. He will also be taking DNA samples from each of you and escorting anyone who needs to relieve themselves to the bathroom. Now, once I have interviewed you, you will be free to go about your business, so long as you do not leave this house without my express permission. Is that understood?"

Everyone nodded, except for Nurse LaFarge, who raised a hand, one of her dark eyebrows arching toward her prominent widow's peak. There was something about the look that suggested he best brace himself.

"Yes?" he said.

"I don't mean to interrupt, but I fear I have detected a logical flaw in these proceedings." She was definitely French, or at least doing a damned good job at a French accent. And to Grave, there was nothing worse than logic wrapped in a French accent, even from a woman as obviously attractive as she was.

"And how is that, miss?"

"You seem to be considering us as suspects, when it is clear that we have been locked in this room all night and could not possibly have stolen the trophy, and therefore have the most rock-solid alibis. It is a matter of pure logic, detective, and in treating us as suspects, you have failed utterly." With that, she puffed her lips into a classic French pout.

Grave took a deep, clearing breath. "Ah, logic is it? Well, Ms. LaFarge, I think you have a grave misunderstanding of logic. It has been my experience that logic is wholly unreliable when it comes to locked-room mysteries. No, what we need to do is wring logic out of the sponge of our understanding and then place that sponge in the waters of the evidence and let it soak up what is true."

"I have no idea what you just said," said LaFarge, "but please consider soaking up this evidence. We are here. The trophy is not. There is only one door in and one door out. Believe me, I've looked for other ways. Therefore, someone who is not us took the trophy, left the room, and then locked us in."

Grave smirked. She had a point, maybe a lot of points, but he wasn't about to let her logic spoil his alternative logic. "And did any of you see another person enter this little room, walk up to the aforementioned trophy, lift it into the air in the presence of all of you, and then walk from the room, locking it behind him?"

No one replied.

"Good. Well, then, let me introduce you to Sergeant Blunt, and we'll begin. I'll just be a moment."

Grave went to the door, then stopped and turned back to ask a final question. He had seen a television detective, Columbo, do this to great effect, and tried to use the technique whenever possible.

"One thing," he said, wishing he were wearing an old trench coat and had at least one eye at odds with the other. "You say you all assembled at 8:00-*ish* last night. Was anyone else supposed to be here, a person or persons who perhaps failed to show up for the unveiling of the MacGuffin Trophy painting?"

Everyone put on their best deep-thought face, most shaking their heads as Whitney stepped forward, nodding and giggling as if she had won a prize.

"Of course! We're missing Piph!"

"Piph?" said Grave.

"Yes, Epiphany Jones, my art dealer and sometime lover," said Whitney.

Grave took a step closer to Whitney. "And could you describe her for me?"

"Of course. She's a little shorter than me, blond to near platinum, eyes bluer than blue, skin as pale as alabaster, with thighs so smooth they melt me to my core."

"I see," said Grave, already imagining them wrapped around each other, flagrante delicto. "And did she have two hands the last time you saw her?"

"Oh, wonderful, wonderful hands," she began in reverie, then stopped with a start. "Well, of course she did. Am I missing something?"

"Perhaps. At any rate, we'll discuss Ms. Jones further when we meet in the library."

He scanned the room. "All right, then, let me bring in Sergeant Blunt."

He moved to the door and slipped out of the room. Sergeant Blunt was standing there next to the door, or at least Grave thought he was.

"Blunt, is that you?" he said.

"Yes, of course," Blunt said, his voice seeming to come from an unexpected direction.

"Well, here's the deal. The people in there are unaware of the murder. They think a trophy has been stolen. Do nothing to make them think otherwise, and keep your eyes and ears open. I've told them not to talk among themselves, but my guess is that they will forget you're there, and open up. Also, check the walls for any possible secret passageways. Do you have the DNA kits?"

"Yes, of course," said a voice behind him.

Grave spun around. "Good. Oh, one thing more. If anyone needs to use the bathroom, you are to escort them. The last thing we need is suspects disappearing left and right, let alone little puddles and piles in every corner."

"No problem," said the voice from behind him once more.

"Dammit, Blunt, stay in one place, will you?"

"Yes, sir," said the same voice in more or less the same direction.

"All right, then, let's go in."

Grave opened the door wide, and they walked in, Blunt's feet flapping noticeably on the floor, which was not unexpected. Sergeant Blunt was an ordinary man in every respect except for his feet, which were also quite ordinary except for their size, which was midway between size 12 1/2 and size 13, leaving him little choice but to wear shoes too big and flap down the street like a clown, or too small and walk as if he were dancing with an invisible ballerina.

Today he was clearly a clown, not that many people would notice, because the fact was that he was not just ordinary, he was nondescript to the point of near invisibility. When he walked into the room, everyone realized the door had opened and something had changed in the room, but they would have been hard pressed to say that a man well over six feet and as wide as Frankenstein's monster had entered the room with Grave. Blunt was like the waves of heat you see hovering over a desert highway, there but not there.

His features, such as they were, did nothing to expose him to the world. If you focused on his eyes, which may have been almost any color, you immediately forgot his nose, a small lump of flesh and cartilage more or less in the center of his face, just above his lips, which were razor thin and appeared to blend into his chin in a way that suggested stealth technology was at work.

He had taken full advantage of his invisibility early in his career, when he had served as a Navy Seal, carrying out mission after mission without detection. He was so good, in fact, that he had been recruited by the CIA. Unfortunately for Blunt, and perhaps world peace, the CIA had insisted that he had failed to show up for his interview, even though he had been there all along, the interviewer tapping a pencil on his desk as Blunt tried, and failed, to get his attention.

It took a man with rare skills in detection to even vaguely be aware of Blunt's presence. Grave was just such a man. He had discovered Blunt one night in a local bar, where Blunt was trying his best to pick up women, with predictably miserable results. Grave had watched in amazement as a woman sidled up to the barstool Blunt was sitting on, and thinking it empty, slowly nudged him off the stool with her hips. In truth, this hip action was Blunt's only brush with sex, and the principal reason he went to bars. In short, if "invisibility" was a game of checkers, Blunt would have been the checker that had fallen to the floor and rolled under the couch, never to be seen again.

But that was neither here nor there, since they were now here not there, and a roomful of people were now staring at them, or at least at Detective Grave, and wondering what was afoot. Grave cleared his throat and pointed to the flickering image of a man standing next to him.

"This is Sergeant Blunt," he said. "He'll be helping me with the case."

Grave took a step toward the door, and turned back again. He really loved this technique. "One last thing. If I should ever speak with a British accent, please let me know by raising your hand."

Everyone raised their hands.

"Oh, dear," he said. He made a mental note to schedule a special appointment with his therapist. These lapses in accent had to stop.

5

The library was just as he had imagined it would be, a square box of a room, or rather a cube, with wraparound book shelves floor to ceiling. It even had ladders that ran on rails to provide easy access to any volume, although the ladder rungs appeared dusty and little used. And although he couldn't imagine Mr. Hawthorne reading a book, the shelves were chockablock with books of every description, all arranged alphabetically by author in sections devoted to various genres, most notably, sailing. A large walnut desk, its top empty but for a small, green-shaded lamp and a set of gold pens put there for show, sat in front of the window, facing into the room and at two burgundy leather chairs.

Smithers had apparently drawn back the heavy red curtains and cracked the windows to provide some fresh air. Even so, the room was redolent with the smell of the decaying pages and words of a thousand authors, mixed with the heady aroma of fresh-brewed coffee, the combined effect of which was intoxicating. Sunlight streamed into the room, dust motes dancing in the air as he walked to the desk, creating what looked like whorls and swirls of fairy dust, but it was just ordinary, run of the mill mansion dust.

Grave swept a handkerchief across the seat of the tall-backed executive chair and sat down behind the desk. So this was what it was like to be the lord of the manor. That thought quickly vanished as Smithers walked into the room, carrying what looked like a cafeteria tray topped with tall stacks of little sandwiches and small, powdery doughnuts.

Grave had to give Hawthorne and Ramrod Robotics their due: Smithers looked every inch a real man, albeit a man burdened with the duties of a butler. The engineers had contrived to build him to be tall and imposing, yet slumpingly deferential. Grave could not detect a single feature that suggested robotics was at work, save perhaps for red cufflinks that pulsed slowly like the turn signals of a car.

Smithers' face resembled someone famous, although Grave could not quite come up with the name. An actor, perhaps. Whomever the model or inspiration, the face was clearly Hollywood handsome, with perfect blue eyes below perfectly carved brows, which he had noticed earlier, could move independently, adding incredible nuance to his expressions. His nose was a work of art, neither too large nor too small, with a pleasing aspect to it and positioned perfectly above lips that could handle more emotions than an emoji. His hair was straight and sandy blonde, and looked quite humanlike. He was, on the whole, better than human.

Smithers set the tray down on a small table next to the desk, where he had already positioned pots of coffee and tea, a small porcelain pitcher of cream, and a silver bowl of sugar, together with the necessary cups and spoons that would be needed for the interviews.

"Will there be anything else, sir?" he said. Grave could have been mistaken, but the voice sounded eerily like the voice of the late Richard Burton, and suitably British.

"Yes, thank you," Grave said. "A couple of things. First, I asked my assistant, Sergeant Blunt, to escort people to the bathroom. Would you mind taking over that job? I think it best that Blunt stay in place and monitor the group."

"Of course, sir."

"Second, I was wondering if your programming includes the ability to record what you see and hear."

Smithers cocked his head to one side as if deep in thought. "Hmm," he said, or at least that's what Grave thought he said. It could have just been a humming noise.

The humming, or perhaps the hmming, stopped. "My programming has been updated from Series 1 to Series 2, which added auditory capability if requested. Otherwise, I only record video. So, yes, I do have that capability, sir. Why do you ask?"

"Wonderful. If you don't mind, I'd like you to sit in on each of the interviews, so that I might call on you at a later date to provide the exact words used by each person." Grave wondered briefly whether a robot's testimony would hold any weight in court.

"I can do that, sir."

"Excellent. Let's begin. Please escort Nurse LaFarge to this room."

"Certainly, sir, but how can I both escort people to the bathroom while remaining here?"

He had a point. "Tell you what. Take the time you need to escort people to the bathroom, and then escort Ms. LaFarge here. While you're doing that, I'll pop down to talk to the medical examiner."

Smithers seemed alarmed. "Medical examiner? Why is there a medical examiner here? I thought we were talking about a missing trophy?"

"Oh, yes, yes, yes," said Grave, trying to get the cat back in the bag. "We're definitely here about the trophy. It's a weekend, you see, and we needed DNA kits, and the ME happened to be in the neighborhood, so—"

Smithers interrupted. "So there's been a murder." It was a statement, not a question.

"Yes," said Grave. "Yes, there's been a murder."

"May I tell the others?"

"No, that would not be a good idea."

Smithers shrugged. "Okee dokee. I'll see to the tasks and meet you back here in, say, twenty minutes?"

Grave sighed, relieved, while at the same time marveling at the words *okee dokee* spoken in the rounded, mellifluous baritone of Richard Burton, a man who could make any shambles of a sentence sound Shakespearean. "Yes, that would be perfect."

Smithers turned on his heels with a barely detectable whir, and marched from the room.

As soon as the door closed, Grave was on his feet and greedily stuffing his mouth with donuts and the little sandwiches, which seemed to involve crab and coarse brown mustard, with a hint of Old Bay seasoning.

6

Grave bolted down the long staircase, the image of the medical examiner growing larger and larger as he descended for what seemed to be an interminable length of time before arriving at the bottom, bent over, hands on knees, gasping for breath.

Polk, who seemed to be watching him with amusement, was wrapping things up, literally. The body had been tagged and bagged and was now being rolled out to a waiting CSI van for transport to the morgue. All that remained was a taped outline of the body on the staircase.

Polk came over and patted Grave on the back. "Are you all right? I can see getting winded running up the steps, but *down?*"

Grave nodded, took one last gasp, and slowly stood upright.

"Oh, my god!" screamed Polk. "What's happened?"

Grave was gravely confused. "What?"

"Your face, that white powder all over your face. Good god, man, are you into cocaine?"

Grave quickly scrubbed at his mouth and wiped away the powder on his chest. "Oh, that. Just sugar donuts."

He wasn't sure whether Polk's expression involved acceptance, dismay, suspicion, or a whole host of other catalogued expressions, but his face *was* contorted in a way intended to more or less express *something*, although he was not being the least bit clear.

Grave ignored him and got right to the point. "So, what do you have so far?"

"Well, as you've probably surmised," he began, "the only trauma to the body was the severed hand. No indications of intercourse, if you were wondering about that. And I won't know cause of death until I can get her back on the table and have a look-see, but I suspect she simply bled out, although there is not enough blood here to indicate that."

"So she was killed somewhere else and then moved here?"

"In all probability. No clothes to be found, so . . ."

Grave nodded. "And the time of death?"

"Body temperature and degree of rigor indicate sometime between 7:00 p.m. and 11:00 p.m. last night."

"I see," said Grave. "When will you be able to tell me more?"

Polk sighed. "You people always want things fast, don't you? Well, you'll just have to wait till Monday. It's a goddam weekend, Grave, or have you forgotten that?"

Grave was miffed. So miffed, in fact, that his next words came out in what Polk would later characterize as a "snarl" when he told his story again and again to the boys back at the morgue. In any event, the words had the effect of forcing Polk to take a step backward to protect his safety from the potential arc of a fast-moving fist.

"You. Will. Have. Results. To. Me. Today!" Grave snarled.

Polk nodded quickly. "As you wish, as you wish."

"Good. Now, I have to get back upstairs to interview the suspects. I'll be expecting your call forthwith."

He turned away from Polk and began running up the stairs, his speed quickly decreasing to a trot and then a poorly done lope and then no more than a slow trudge, and he was only halfway up.

Polk called up to him, his voice seemingly miles away. "You know, you could have taken the elevator."

7

Lola LaFarge was already seated when Grave huffed and puffed his way back into the room. Smithers was standing at attention just inside the room in a way that suggested unobtrusiveness and stealth, with the modicum of attentiveness you would expect from a tape recorder.

Grave sat down behind the desk, ran a hand through his hair, and waited for his heart rate to slow to a point that would suggest the heart of a man and not that of a bird. He considered the woman seated across from him, sipping at a cup of coffee, her mouth and cheeks coated with powdered sugar.

"Those doughnuts are good, are they not?" he said.

LaFarge raised her hand.

"You have a question?"

"No, you said to raise my hand if you lapsed into a British accent."

"Oh, sorry. There, is this better?"

LaFarge smiled, but in a way that seemed incredibly arrogant, even for a person with a French accent.

One of Grave's theories was that a person's level of arrogance was inversely proportional to their height, which clearly held true for Ms. LaFarge, who was diminutive beyond petite.

She was also strikingly beautiful. Her chestnut brown hair was done up in one of those whatchamacallit hairdos that was cut short in back and left long in front, giving the impression that her head was accelerating toward you at great speed, like some planet-killing asteroid. But the effect seemed to suit her, and had the further effect of emphasizing her large eyes, which were brown, somewhere between walnut and hazelnut, and came with thin eyebrows that had been shaped and plucked to near nonexistence. They reminded him of the v-shaped birds in children's paintings, except these were flying upside down and lending a surprised look to Ms. LaFarge.

There was not much to say about her body except that it was perfect in every way. Her breasts, full and round and threatening to pop out of her deep-cut red sweater, were exemplars of breasts done right, perky and creamy smooth. The rest of her body had decided long ago to play along with the perfection of her breasts, providing the counterpoint of a slender waist, ample hips, and an ass to die for, all held upright by legs not even Michelangelo could improve upon, which today were clearly defined by black yoga pants that left little to the imagination. In short, if "beautiful" was a box of assorted chocolates, she would have been the one you were hoping to find before anyone else did.

And now she was moving her full, pouty lips in a manner that suggested she was speaking to him. Her small, upturned nose wiggled with each word, as if it didn't want to be left out of the conversation.

"Did you not hear me?" she said, wiggling her nose and waving a hand to get his attention, causing him to break his reverie.

"Of course, mademoiselle," he said, then worried whether he was being too flirtatious. He stumbled on. "What did you say again?"

"I said, why the *fuck* didn't you tell us that Piph has been dead on the staircase the whole time you've been here?"

Grave glanced quickly at Smithers, who sheepishly turned his head away.

"Um," he began and knew in an instant that "um" was never a good way to begin a conversation you hoped to control.

She continued, ignoring his prefatory um. "Well, there's complete pandemonium back in the studio. Poor Whitney is beside herself. You should have posted an officer there to keep things in hand."

"I did. Sergeant Blunt."

"Who?"

"Blunt." He could see she was completely mystified. "Never

mind. Just know that I had my reasons."

She rolled her eyes. "Like you have your reasons to ignore logic and interrogate us when you should be letting us go so we can grieve for poor Ms. Jones."

The sentence came out so quickly there was no need for commas, and gave Grave little time to formulate a worthy response. In such situations, he found it effective to form his hands into a tent, finger to finger, and flex them slightly to create in the observer an image of a spider crawling up a mirror, and thus distract them, if only for a few seconds.

"My apologies. I thought by denying you and the others this information, I might glean a clue or two about the killer, whom I am sure is one of you, the people locked in that room all night."

"And did you *glean* anything about me?" she said defiantly, head thrust toward him, her widow's peak slashing toward him like a weapon. A fine spray of spittle made it all the way to his hands, which he then dropped to his lap and inconspicuously wiped on his trousers.

"No, not really. When I went along with this MacGuffin Trophy nonsense, I was hoping to detect a 'tell.' Are you familiar with that term, Ms. LaFarge?"

She shook her head.

"A *tell* is an inappropriate or unexpected response to a situation. A small behavior that the person is not aware of, but that reveals something about that person."

"I'm not sure I follow you."

"Okay, so let's use the trophy as an example. When I reacted in a way that suggested I was definitely there to deal with the purloined trophy, everyone but the killer, of course, would have behaved normally. The killer, on the other hand, would have reacted with a *tell*, an involuntary and telling response—a surprised look, a turning away, a sly smile, an inadvertent request for clarification—*something* out of the ordinary. And that was what I was looking for."

"And did you see such a tell?"

He started to answer but she held up a hand to stop him.

"Non! You didn't see a tell at all. You saw nothing, am I right? And you saw nothing because there is no logical way for a person locked in a room all night to kill a person outside that room, or even steal a damned fucking trophy."

Grave had had enough.

"Ms. LaFarge, I am not about to discuss my techniques or what I did or did not glean from our first meeting. Suffice to say that I have reason to believe that one of you is, in fact, the murderer."

Ms. LaFarge slumped back into her chair, clearly exasperated, and crossed her arms under her breasts, pushing them up to briefly reveal the outer rim of her aureoles, which were just slightly darker than her skin, with a slight pink blush.

She caught him looking.

"So, monsieur detective, what are you gleaning now?"

Grave looked away and fumbled with his notebook, not that there was anything in his notebook about her except one brief, hurriedly scrawled note: "Wow!"

That analysis continued to hold sway as he put her through a series of questions about her background and her role in the mansion. She had emigrated from France two years previously with the promise of a job at the Hawthorne mansion, to provide daily nursing assistance to Edwina Hawthorne while home schooling young Roy Lynn Waters, the erstwhile Indian chief and incorrigible son of Whitney Waters. In those two years, Edwina remained wheelchair-bound and sullen, and Roy Lynn had developed a French accent.

Like the others, she had gone to the studio at precisely eight-*ish* to see Whitney's painting of the trophy. The event went smoothly, Whitney revealing the painting to polite applause and ample champagne. Ms. LaFarge, who was not keen on Whitney's painting style had hoped to slip away at 8:30, but that hope ended when Whitney had checked the door, finding it locked. There then followed a near comical attempt by everyone in the room to "try" the door, which continued to remain locked despite everyone's best efforts to think otherwise.

"And why did it take so long to notify the police?" he asked.

"I know it's ridiculous in this day and age, but not a single one of us had a cellphone with us."

"So how did you notify us? Surely not with the insane knocking I experienced when I first arrived."

"No, just before daybreak we remembered, or rather Mr. Hawthorne remembered, that Smithers here is equipped with Wi-Fi and has a drop-down keyboard in his back."

Grave turned to Smithers. "Is that correct?"

Smithers nodded. "Yes, sir, that is correct. And the time of the email message was exactly 6:56 a.m."

"And why didn't you offer that service immediately upon learning that the room was locked?"

Grave thought he heard the soft screeching of tiny gears or perhaps an ill-timed release of robotic gasses.

"Well, sir," said Smithers, "no one asked. And I thought it would be intrusive of me, nay inappropriate for me as a butler, to offer unsolicited guidance to my masters."

Grave made a note of that, and also wondered why it had taken nearly three hours for anyone at the precinct to notify him.

"Thank you, Smithers," he said, turning his attention back to Ms. LaFarge, who had apparently been studying him as he spoke to Smithers, her eyes quickly averted when he looked back at her. He noticed that her neck and chest were now flushed in a way that, in Grave's experience, indicated one of three things: anger, nervousness, or arousal. He was hoping for the third option.

"Now, Ms. LaFarge, at any time during this hours-long detention did anyone act either overly dramatic about the situation, or perhaps just the opposite, an almost carefree acceptance of your combined plight?"

She considered the question briefly, and gave him an impish shrug. "Not particularly."

Grave sat in silence for some moments, which apparently was enough time for Ms. LaFarge to formulate a question or two.

"Detective, can I ask you a personal question?"

"I don't see why not," he said, "but I may reserve the right not to answer it."

"Of course," she said. "I was just wondering about this man-about-the-docks getup you're wearing. It doesn't seem to suit you."

"Ah," he began, hoping that in that "ah" he could disguise his true reason for wearing his Italian gigolo duds, namely to pick up women. "I was on a stakeout, at that little café, surely you know the one, Le

Crabe Bleu, down by the marina."

"A stakeout? For what?"

"Drugs," he lied. "We have reason to believe that someone has been bringing in cocaine and heroin in boxes of salt shakers."

"So you were hoping to catch some sort of financial transaction between a waiter and a customer requesting salt?"

"Well . . ."

"Oui, I see it now. The drug dealer comes to the café and looks for the one table that does not have a salt shaker. He sits down, places an order, and when it comes, he pretends to notice he has no salt, which the waiter, who's in on the whole thing and wears a black eye patch by way of identification, brings to him, with some sort of exchange for money, perhaps folded bills quickly placed into the waiter's palm, or maybe even a briefcase left behind, or—"

Grave had to stop her before she wrote an entire case file. "Yes, that's it exactly."

She sat back in her chair, tapped a finger aside her nose, and then rolled her hand in his direction. "So this is not your normal attire?"

"No, it's—"

"Hush," she said. "Don't tell me. I have a nose for this." Indeed, her nose was wiggling like a bloodhound's.

She looked him up and down, her nose sniffing appraisingly. "Hmm, okay, my guess is that you usually wear a suit. No vest, of course, that would be too British, and you'd just lapse into that terrible accent. And the suit would be gray. No, not just gray—*only* gray. You have a closet full of gray suits, lined up one after another, for each day of the week, am I right?"

"Um," he offered.

"Ha, I knew it!" she beamed. "But there's more. All your shirts are white, with button-down collars, and you prefer thin, solid ties, mostly a darker gray, but never black."

"Well, I do have a Christmas tie."

"Doesn't count," she giggled. "Now, as to shoes, I'm thinking black walking shoes with spongy soles, because you like the way they let you slip into the precinct undetected."

Grave was beginning to become uncomfortable with this spot-on analysis. "Shall we get back to the subject at hand? I have a number of questions for you about Ms. Jones."

"We can, but first you have to admit that I'm right."

"Very well," he said, flipping his notebook to a new page. "Yes, you're right. Now, if we can continue."

"Of course," she said, trying her best to put on the nervous expression of a murder suspect, but failing utterly, a burst of laughter coming from her that was deep and genuine, and to Grave's mind, intriguingly sexual. "Did I mention, how do you say, your tighty whities?"

Grave tried to gather himself, but he could sense that his face was working its way through various hues of red, and would have reached full-on crimson if it had not been for the door bursting open, all the other suspects rushing in like angry villagers on the hunt for a monster, albeit without torches and pitchforks.

Among the mélange of outrage and insults being shouted his way, he could detect the small voice of Sergeant Blunt, who was there somewhere.

"Sorry, sir."

A suction-cupped arrow whizzed by Grave's head, signaling the end of the day's interviews. He pushed through the villagers and rushed outside.

8

Grave stepped out of the mansion to what looked like a carnival setting up outside, television trucks from the local television stations already positioned on the mansion lawn, a host of reporters dressed to the nines already illuminated in lights, cameramen dressed to the ones following their every move.

Grave picked up the pace, hoping to avoid Claire Fairly, the crime reporter from Channel 3, a woman whose annoying persistence was the hallmark of her professional life. By the time he reached his car, he had managed to locate her. She had spotted him and was racing toward his car, trailed by her cameraman, who was struggling to keep up.

Fortunately, she wasn't able to close the distance fast enough, Grave driving away proudly and quickly in his Lamborghini Miura P-400S, at least in his imagination, which had Smithers waving goodbye to him and repeating his dream car's name over and over as only Richard Burton could. The reality of the situation was that he was driving away in his actual, real-life car, an old 1965 Austin Healey Sprite sports convertible, a gift from his now-retired father, which was pretty much a beginner sports car, a bottom feeder in the sporting class, more of a roller skate than an actual vehicle.

He had slipped his tall frame into the little red car, which was no more than four breadbaskets wide by nine breadbaskets long, a feat that required him to stretch his legs out full length in order to reach the pedals for the clutch, brakes, and accelerator. One of his old girlfriends, who had eventually run away with a tuba player, said that when he was finally seated in the car, he looked like a man sitting upright in his own coffin, with the same startling effect to passersby, a driving position that perhaps only the British could appreciate, the body jackknifed at a right angle, legs stretched out, derriere just six inches off the ground.

The only good thing that could be said about this position was that it created a speed-thrill effect that was quite exhilarating. At twenty miles an hour, you felt like you were going sixty; at sixty, you were quite sure you were approaching escape velocity; and at eighty, near the end of the speedometer's range, you were not only willing to accept the possibility of time travel, you were absolutely convinced that Marty McFly's trip back to the future actually happened.

As he sped away, Fairly becoming smaller and smaller in his rearview mirror, the radio came on simultaneously, stuck as always on Radio 780 AM, a Christian station featuring gospel music and the one-minute hourly reflections of Reverend Bendigo Bottoms, who this hour was in the middle of a sermon on one of his many Eleventh Commandments, in this case, "Thou shalt not rage in the road."

Over the many months he had owned the car, Grave had come to appreciate gospel music and the reverend, but in keeping with the day's commandment, but not observing it, he pounded on the radio several times before giving up and continuing down the lane to the gate, where he turned right and accelerated away from the mansion.

He had managed to calm everyone down by releasing them for the rest of the day, with the stipulation that he would return early the next morning to continue his interrogations. Most seemed satisfied with that solution, but he could still see the look Whitney had given him as he left the room, a look that wrapped anger, hurt, betrayal, and grief into a massive ball and hurled it at his head with the words, "You bastard!"

He glanced at his watch, an oversized Timex with more functions than a convention center. It read 49:57, which could have been the exact time on a distant planet, but was in fact the reading from the chronometer function for the watch, and clearly of no help. He fumbled with the watch as he drove, trying to stay on his side of the road as he pushed various combinations of buttons, none of which resulted in the display of the current time. He would have to rely on the position of the sun in the sky and the direction and length of shadows to determine an approximate time. The result of these calculations was that to his best estimation it was daylight.

He drove on, hoping that Polk would still be at the morgue, poking and probing poor Epiphany Jones. Traffic was relatively light, even for a weekend, so he made good time, walking into Polk's examination room at just after daylight, which inexplicably was still daylight. He quickly fixed the watch to discover that it was, in fact, 1:37 in the afternoon, which clearly explained the renewed rumbling of his stomach, which had had its fill of tiny sandwiches and powdered donuts, and wanted more, much more.

Polk hovered over the body, talking into a headset microphone. He caught sight of Grave and motioned him over, continuing his analysis. The smell of the place was somewhere between rotten and cloyingly sweet, and it was all that Grave could do to fight back a looming gag reflex. How did Polk do this day after day?

". . . and a small puncture wound through the intercostal muscles, between the third and fourth ribs, just to the left of the spine." He took the headset off and dropped it on a nearby tray.

"You should have a look at this, detective."

Grave walked over and looked down at the body, which was working its way through various shades of gray, and had a waxy look about it. It, or rather she, had been beautiful in life, even from the backside, or perhaps especially from the back side, her back the kind of back a woman would want to display in a backless gown, her waist narrowing, then expanding seductively to hips that tried their best to contain an ass that could only have been shaped with the help of a professional trainer.

Polk cleared his throat to end Grave's obvious reverie, then tapped the puncture wound on the woman's back with a gloved finger. "Here, you see, a devilishly precise kill, through the rib cage and angled slightly to pierce the heart. I dare say, the work of a professional, or at least someone with more than a passing knowledge of anatomy and icepicks. That, or just blind luck. Or rather, *misfortune* for poor Ms. Jones."

"Icepicks?" said Grave. "Who the hell uses icepicks these days?"

"A small list, to be sure. Bartenders, perhaps, or more likely, ice sculptors or trained assassins. Of course, the murderer could have used a knitting needle."

Grave quickly reviewed his list of suspects, Whitney Waters coming immediately to mind, but only because she was an artist. Did she do ice sculptures, he wondered. As for knitters, he didn't have a purl of a clue. On the other hand, this new revelation gave him a wealth of potential questions for tomorrow's interrogations.

"What about the hand? Any clue how or when it was severed?"

"I would say post mortem, given how clean the cut is. A butcher's saw, perhaps, or maybe the band saw of a woodworker."

"Why on earth would someone do that?"

Polk shook his head. "The larger question, of course, is why he left the hand at the scene? Was he sending a message to someone?"

"Or was he leaving behind one trophy in exchange for the one he had just stolen, the MacGuffin Trophy."

"An interesting thought, detective."

Grave made a few quick notes in his notebook. "Anything else, Polk?"

Polk shrugged. "Not for a while. I'm really just beginning. Are you going to be at home or should I reach you on your cell?"

"My cell. I dropped the land line months ago. It just seemed so twentieth century."

"All right, then, I'll give you a call when I'm done here."

Grave nodded, looked down at the body once more, and left the room. As the doors swung shut behind him, he could hear Polk talking to the body.

"Let's open you up, my lovely, and see what's what."

9

Grave was ravenous. He didn't know whether it was from the passage of time or the time he had spent at the morgue. Death had a way of reminding you that any meal could be your last, so best go at it full tilt. That thought had quickly brought him to Luigi's Trattoria and Crab House for the kind of crabby Italian meal that leaves a smile on your face and your stomach rounded to a belt-stretching fullness.

He grabbed a handful of mints on the way out, and headed for his father's place. He had promised him a visit, and this new case would provide ample fodder for conversation.

Jacob Grave was nestled in his electric recliner, which was equipped with all the necessary accessories required to minimize movement and encourage gluttony. It even had cup holders and a small under-arm refrigerator large enough to hold a six-pack of beer and a package of cheese sticks. An oversized bag of pretzels was stuffed beside him, a snack that would carry him to dinner, which would be carried to him by the food service he employed for this purpose.

Had he stood up, you would have encountered a 74-year-old man who was once tall and robust, but who had now become withered and hunched, with spindly legs that could barely take him to the bathroom and back. His hair, once thick and wavy like Simon's, had all but left him, leaving the impression that you were looking at a worn white bowling ball with ice blue rheumy eyes. Simon shuddered every time he looked at him, his future self, his father no longer the master detective he once was, the pride of the precinct. In short, if "decrepit" was a forest, old man Grave would have been one of the fallen trees rotting on its floor.

The television was blaring as usual, so Simon picked up the controller and pushed the mute button.

"What the fuck!" his father said. "Oh, it's you. Dammit, could you at least announce yourself when you come through the fucking door? You liked to killed me."

Simon handed the controller back to his father. "Sorry, I thought you heard me."

"Hearing is going, I guess, along with everything else." He clicked the controller and the image of a pitchman selling "miracle gloves" imploded to nothingness.

"Now, what brings you here on a bright Saturday afternoon? You should be out cruising for chicks. Lord knows, from the look of you, you could use a good fuck or six."

Grave sighed. "Working a new case. Thought you might like to hear about it?"

"Maybe," he said with a hint of interest. The man may retire, but not the detective in him. He flipped open the arm of the chair and pulled out a beer. "Want one?"

"No, a bit early, and I'm stuffed to the gills. In fact, I brought you a doggie bag of crab linguini from Luigi's."

His father perked up. "Luigi's? Damn, how can you afford Luigi's on your salary?" He dropped the beer back in and flipped the arm closed. "Not that I'm complaining, mind. Best damn food on the planet, save for your poor mother's, rest her soul."

This was the first time he had mentioned Grave's mother in the three years since her death, from cancer.

Simon put a hand on his father's shoulders. "Have you been to her grave recently?"

His father shrugged the hand off, writhing as if touched by something otherworldly. "No, and I don't plan to, either."

"Why not?"

"It's just so depressing. All those graves, and those fucking flowers. Who thinks killing flowers is what the dead want?"

"It's a tradition, Dad."

"Well, fuck tradition, and while you're at it, fuck those fucking *fake* flowers, too. What does it say about someone who is so inconvenienced by visiting that they would leave permanent flowers of their plastic affection?"

Simon now deeply regretted even mentioning his mother, but knew that he would have to ride out this tirade.

"And here's the kicker. Do you know what really keeps me away from her grave?"

Simon did not even have time to open his mouth before his father charged on.

"I'll tell you what, it's because every single time I go there, some stranger's kids are hovering over her gravestone, laughing their heads off and screaming, 'Oh, look, this is the grave of a Grave.'"

Simon had no intelligent response to that, so he quickly changed the subject. "Let me just get a plate for this linguini. You look hungry."

His father shook his head. "No, I've had my fill of cheese sticks and pretzels, which I'll regret later when I try to take a dump. Just put the bag in the ice box, and I'll get it later. The exercise will do me good. Look at me, I've become a marshmallow held up by toothpicks."

Simon said nothing, going immediately to the kitchen, which looked like it had barely survived an explosion of dishes and food scraps. He made his way across the floor, dodging banana peels and empty Styrofoam boxes from Speedy Meals, and opened the refrigerator, which smelled a lot like the morgue, only worse. A moldy loaf of bread appeared to move. He tossed the bag in and retreated to the living room, carefully avoiding food mines along the way.

His father had taken advantage of the time to wrestle himself to his feet and move to the card table he now used for endless games of solitaire and an occasional nostalgic walk down memory lane with a folder or two of documents he had copied from the case files of murders that had gone unsolved on his watch, most notably those related to Chester Clink, the Dockside Ripper, a master of disguise and still at large, his father's case for many years and the one that had delayed his retirement more than once.

He motioned Simon to take a seat in the small folding chair he kept handy for the occasional visitor.

"Now, what's this about a new case?"

Simon opened the chair, sat down, and looked at his father, whose entire demeanor had changed, an amazing transformation from near invalid to ace detective, his eyes gleaming, his head cocked to one side, waiting to take in information.

Simon described what had transpired at the mansion earlier in the day, his father perking up noticeably when he heard that Chester Clink's sister, Philomena, was involved.

"Philomena, you say?" His father slapped the table, making it bounce. "She and her brother are like two peas in a pod. Psychopaths, the both of them. You should put her at the top of your list."

"Good to know, Dad, but she seemed rather passive and nondescript, except for her clothing. She's one of those people who love black."

"Ha, that's not nondescript, that's the low-affect look of a serial killer."

Simon was nonplussed. "Wait, you think *she's* a killer as well? Of whom?"

His father waved a bony hand in the air. "Just a theory, just a theory, but I'd keep a close eye on her. If nothing else, it might lead us to the whereabouts of that damned elusive maniac, Chester Fuckin' Clink." He stroked his chin as if he had a beard, an old habit from when he did have a big, black, lumberjack beard. "Several things about the case—my case—suggest that the two were, and perhaps still are, working together."

Simon shook his head. "The details don't fit, Dad, at least in this case—my case. The woman was killed with a single, well-aimed thrust of an icepick or similar instrument."

"An icepick? Who in hell uses an icepick these days?"

"Yeah, I know."

Simon's father cocked his head back and forth a few times, which was his way of processing information, although Simon always imagined his father's brain sloshing from side to side as he did this.

"What about security cameras? Anything there?"

Simon cringed. He'd never asked about security cameras. "Not yet," he said, trying his best to cover up the mistake. His father thankfully let it pass.

"So," his father said finally, "who's working the case with you?"

"Blunt."

"And who's the medical examiner?"

"Polk."

"Oh, sweet Jesus, boy, you're working with invisible and incompetent? I feel for you, I truly do."

Their review of the case went on for some minutes, each agreeing to contact the other if anything of interest turned up. Finally, he walked his father back to his recliner and eased him down.

"Thanks for coming, son." He fumbled around for the remote.

"No problem, it was good to see you, and you know how much I value your thoughts on my cases."

"Well, I like to think I still have a nose for it." He clicked on the television, putting it on mute as Columbo walked across the screen in his signature trench coat.

"You do, you do."

His father gave him an odd, appraising look. "Before you go, there's one other thing."

"Okay, shoot."

"What's with the British accent? I thought you'd kicked that habit."

Simon sighed. "Shit, I thought I had, too."

"I know how this goes, son. There was a time early in my career when I did exactly the same thing. It's about confidence, or a lack thereof. I mean, anything a sophisticated Brit says sounds true, right?"

Simon nodded. "They could say up is down, and everyone would believe them."

"It lends them an air of authority that apparently you don't think you have."

"Maybe."

"No, without a doubt. It's a confidence thing, and you need to suck it up and trust yourself and your instincts. You don't need this British accent thing. For one thing, it makes people think you're peculiar."

"I know, I've seen the looks."

"On the other hand, I know it's compelling. Hell, if I could give advice to any perp facing trial, I'd say, I don't care how guilty you are, use a British accent when you're on the stand, and you'll have a good chance of going free."

They both laughed, then grew silent for an uncomfortable period. Finally, his father slapped his hands on both arms of the chair. "Well, then, you best get back to your case."

The air outside was the freshest and most invigorating in the world compared to the stale, moldy atmosphere of his father's living room. His cell phone rang the minute he had nestled himself in his car.

"Grave? Polk, here. You'd better get back here."

Grave definitely didn't want to go back to the morgue, although considering the state of his father's place, it would be a step up in air quality.

"Why? What've you got?" He could hear Polk's exasperated sigh on the other end of the line.

"All right, don't come back. I just thought you'd like to see this first hand."

"See what?"

"Oil, traces of oil in the wound channel and the heart."

"Oil? What kind of oil?" This case was getting odder by the minute.

"Not sure yet. We're running some tests. Should know by tomorrow morning, I think."

"Okay, I'll stop by first thing and have a look."

Grave was expecting Polk to object or say some kind of goodbye, but the line was silent.

He waited a few seconds more. "Polk, are you there?"

"Yes, it's just . . ." His voice trailed off.

"Polk, is there something you're not telling me?"

The sigh sounded like the first gust of wind in an approaching storm, not strong enough to knock you off your feet, but strong enough to alert you that you best get indoors.

"It's about the hand."

"The severed hand?"

"Yes."

"Well, what about it?"

"By any chance, did you take it with you when you left?" He sounded incredibly sheepish.

"What? Of course not."

"I thought so. Well, you see, the thing is, it's gone missing."

Grave shook his head in disbelief. Maybe his father was right about Polk.

10

Grave and Blunt arrived at the morgue at precisely 37:45 the next morning, according to Grave's watch at least. Blunt thought the time was more like 7:37, which Grave accepted without further comment.

Both men seemed to have read the same memo, each of them dressed in a gray suit, white shirt, and thin gray tie, but only one of them fully visible to Polk, who wondered about the gray blur next to Grave. He blinked a couple of times, and the blur disappeared entirely.

"Good morning, detective."

Two voices, one from Grave and one apparently an echo, said good morning back at him.

"Oh, I'm sorry, I didn't see you at first, Sergeant Blunt."

"No problem," Blunt said.

"Let's get to it, then," said Grave. "I need to get back to the Hawthorne mansion."

Polk took a deep breath and got to it. "Other than the missing hand, which we still haven't found, we have this oil. Look here." He motioned them to a stainless steel table against the wall, and pointed at a small Petri dish containing a few drops of a clear liquid.

"We were able to isolate it and run a few tests."

Grave was impatient. "Yes, yes, what is it, then?"

"Machine oil."

"You mean like for a sewing machine, or something?"

Polk shook his head vigorously. "Oh, no. Much more refined than that. The very finest, in fact. This is the kind of oil you'd use on a precision instrument, where tolerances are tight and viscosity can become a real issue. It's called protoglycothanitine, or proto for short, and you can thank our space program for it."

Grave was thrilled to have a clue. "And it was in the wound channel, you say?"

"Yes, and a few drops in the heart itself."

"Curious," said Grave. "Perhaps we're looking for something other than an icepick."

"I'd have to agree," said Polk. "A machine part of some kind, perhaps."

Grave turned to Blunt, or at least thought he had. "Blunt, check out sources for this oil and any local customers."

"Yes, sir," said a voice from across the room, in the general direction of the table occupied by the late Ms. Jones. "Over here, sir. I was just wondering about the angles and so forth of the wound."

"Ah," said Polk. "Thanks for reminding me. The icepick, or whatever was used, was thrust in at a fifteen degree upward angle from horizontal, but not with enough force to leave any latent bruising."

"Is there anything about that angle that suggests the height of our killer?" said Grave.

"Unfortunately, no. The victim is only five feet four, so even a child could have pulled off the thrust. Plus, we don't know whether she was standing, sitting, or lying down when she received the thrust."

"What about handedness?" said Blunt, now on the opposite side of the table. "Is he a righty or a lefty?"

"A lefty, I would think," said Polk.

"From the angle of the entry?" asked Grave.

"No, from the happy face painted on her stomach." He turned the body over. "See how the brush stroke swirls and breaks up here?"

Grave and Blunt nodded.

"Only a lefty could do that."

"What about the arrow? Anything from that?" asked Blunt.

"No, not yet. We've sent off the arrow and the DNA to the lab for processing. Should have the results in a couple of weeks. That suction cup should be loaded with evidence."

Grave sighed. "Two weeks? Why does it take so long?"

Polk had to deal with this question every day of his career. "Listen, I must have gone over this with you a hundred times. We're a small town. We don't have our own lab. Have to rely on the folks in Oyster County. So, assuming there's no backlog, and there always is, just the pure lab time takes over fifty hours, and that's not even counting the extensive cleaning that must be done before and after each sequence to assure the accuracy of the testing. And then—"

"Never mind," said Grave. "I was just hoping we could expedite it."

"I'll do what I can," said Polk, but Grave wasn't betting on it.

Grave checked his watch. It was already 43:13, and they'd best be on their way. "And the hand is gone?"

"Yes," said Polk. "I just don't understand it."

"Maybe the killer retrieved it," said Blunt, who was now standing beside them. "I mean, maybe he hadn't intended to leave it at the scene."

Grave nodded. "Yes, perhaps it was his trophy."

"And if that's true, if he's into trophies," said Blunt, apparently already headed for the door, "then we can expect more killings."

Grave thanked Polk with a nod and gave chase, turning at the door. "Check the security cameras, will you?"

Polk nodded. "Yes, I'll give you a call."

Grave turned on his heels and pushed through the door. Time was of the essence, whatever time that happened to be.

11

The drive to the mansion was uneventful, if you consider riding in a squad car with a driver you can barely see uneventful. Grave had heard about driverless cars, and frankly, didn't want anything to do with them. Despite himself, he "braked" several times during the trip. His only hope was to engage Blunt in conversation, if only as a distraction.

"So, what do you think?" said Grave.

"I'm wondering if it might be Smithers."

"Wait, what? You think the butler did it?"

"I know it's a cliché and not something we would want to get around the precinct, but Smithers is a robot, which the last time I checked would be considered a precision instrument."

Grave considered this, and as much as he hated to admit it, the new clue elevated Smithers to the status of prime suspect. Or maybe not. "Possible, perhaps probable, but remember, where there's robots, there's robot parts that anyone could use as a murder weapon."

"Good point. I'll see if I can come up with anything on robot parts that might resemble icepickness. Perhaps Mr. Hawthorne can give us a hand with that."

"I'll ask. He's first up on this morning's interviews."

"I thought you still had questions for Ms. LaFarge."

"I do, but I think I'll save her for last. She's not high on my suspect list." She was high on another list, though, a list that Grave was not about to share with Blunt.

They drove on for some minutes, Grave watching the surprised, dumbfounded looks of pedestrians as they watched what they thought was a driverless car speed by. And then Grave had a thought.

"Wait, aren't robots prohibited from harming humans?"

"You mean the laws of robotics?"

"Yes, Pratchett's Law."

Blunt laughed. "No, Terry Pratchett was a fantasy author, and while he did touch on the laws of robotics and add to them, he did so in a humorous way."

"Heinlein's Law, then."

"No again. Robert Heinlein did write about robots, to be sure, but the author you're thinking of is Isaac Asimov."

Grave was incredulous. "Asimov? No way."

"I know I'm right, sir," said Blunt. "Go ahead and google it."

Grave pulled out his smartphone and did just that. "Um, you seem to be correct." He read the laws to himself:

1. *A robot may not injure a human being or, through inaction, allow a human being to come to harm.*
2. *A robot must obey the orders given it by human beings except where such orders would conflict with the First Law.*
3. *A robot must protect its own existence as long as such protection does not conflict with the First or Second Laws.*

"Ah," said Grave. "I guess this eliminates Smithers."

Blunt's head, or where his head should have been, appeared to blur in a way that would suggest it was shaking back and forth, in a clear, or rather blurry, display of polite objection.

"Two problems. First, we don't know whether the laws were programmed into Smithers, and second, we don't know whether Smithers himself—itself?—believes he's—it's—a robot."

Grave gave Blunt an appreciative glance. "Good thinking."

"Thank you, sir."

Blunt had just pulled through the massive gate in the massive stone wall that encircled the massive estate and the massive mansion that had been constructed with massive effort by a massive force of workers in an era when massive was the order of the day.

"Damn," said Grave. "I didn't get a chance to debrief you on what transpired in that studio while I was interviewing Ms. LaFarge."

A notebook suddenly appeared in front of his face.

"Take my notebook. Not much happened, but here are my notes."

He snatched the book out of midair. "Okay, great. I don't know how long these interviews will last, but give me a call when and if you come across anything interesting. Otherwise, we'll touch base at the end of the day."

"Yes, sir."

The car rolled to a stop, and Grave started to get out, then stopped. "By any chance do you have a ball of some kind?"

If Blunt smiled, it was a smile not even a Cheshire cat could see. "Good thought, sir. Yes, in the glove compartment. An old tennis ball."

Grave opened the glove compartment and everything but gloves poured out into his lap, the worn old tennis ball included. He put the ball in his suit pocket and stuffed everything else back into the glove compartment.

"It's a bit like Dagwood's closet, isn't it?" said Grave.

"Who?"

"Dagwood, from the comics."

"Never heard of him."

Ah, youth, Grave thought. He opened the car door, stepped out, and swung the door closed. Blunt immediately accelerated away, a spray of gravel, the kind that only rich people could afford, striking Grave's shins with stinging authority.

12

The Hawthorne Mansion, a testament to moneyed excess and snooty disregard for architectural periods and styles, sat atop a bluff overlooking the Chesapeake Bay, looking more like a crustaceous carbuncle on the landscape than a home. Its massive, whitewashed brick exterior, a mélange of turrets and towers and discordant angles, created a can't-miss-it beacon and reference point to vessels great and small. From its vantage point, the Hawthornes could keep watch on the bay and the town below, the high bluff falling away toward a near sea-level town of 3,000 permanent residents, most housed in white clapboard homes scrubbed raw by the wind, the sand, and the sea.

The town, Crab Cove, which attracted as many as 15,000 people a day during the summer months, was the invention of an eccentric real estate developer, who saw money in the idea of a planned town midway between the nation's capital to the west and the ocean beaches to the east, a place where beachgoers could stop for a meal on the long ride to or from the beach, or where the moneyed few like the Hawthornes could build extravagant estates with majestic views and private slips for their yachts.

So he had scouted the Eastern Shore of Maryland for the perfect spot, and settled on a tiny town called Little Willy's Landing, a town named after its founder, Sir William Skunkford, whose family had settled the area as "Skunkford" in 1750 with a modest land grant from the king. The good people of Skunkford had changed the name of the town shortly after the American Revolution, the name chosen to disparage Mr. Skunkford's legendary anatomical shortcoming as payback for his support of the crown, as well as to encourage his rapid flight.

Not that the name Skunkford had disappeared entirely. It could still be seen in various forms around town, from the auto dealer Skunk Ford ("We smell a deal") to the donut shop, Skunk 'n Donuts ("Home of the Little Willy Cruller").

The town's main industry was crabbing, which fit perfectly with the developer's plan. What better way to entice travelers than the simple word "crab" and the promise of steamed blue crabs seasoned with Old Bay and piled high on tables covered with the unread pages of the local newspaper, *The Claw & Mallet*? And what better name than Crab Cove, "crab" fulfilling the promise of good eats and "cove" suggesting a place of rest and shelter far away from the drone and weave of beach traffic?

And so the developer had bought up the town, creating a main street of shops and restaurants featuring all things crab. Most businesses renamed themselves, inserting "crab" into their names to match the spirit of the town. If you wanted a beer, you went to The Drunken Crab or the Blue Fin Grill. If you wanted a book, you went to the bookstore, Claw-Claw-Clawdius Books. And if you wanted crabs, well, you could find them at Bob's Crab Shack, the Crab Cove Market, or the very upscale Le Crabe Bleu. And if you were in a hurry, Cal's Crab Truck could set you up with a bushel of fresh-caught blues to keep you company on the trip home.

Billboards went up on all points of the compass, and the people came and kept on coming, bringing money but also money's evil siblings, greed and crime.

None of this history was of the slightest interest to Detective Simon Grave as he raced up the mansion's steps, through a sea of cameras and microphones, Claire Fairly in hot pursuit, shouting out as many questions as she could before he disappeared through the mansion's doors, leaving her in a sea of her own expletives.

The suspects had apparently been watching them come up the drive, because as soon as Grave reached the mansion's front doors, which complied completely with the massiveness theme, the heavy doors swung open in a way he imagined the gates of Troy had opened to receive the Trojan horse, with a mixture of drunken jubilance and muted apprehension.

Smithers stood in front of the gathered suspects, bent slightly at the waist.

"Welcome, sir," he said. "We've prepared the drawing room just off the foyer for your interviews. If you'd like a full breakfast, you may join us in the dining room, where a massive buffet awaits your every desire."

As much as he would have liked to follow the near visible aroma of bacon and butter into the dining room, he opted to stand fast. He shook his head and scanned the assembled suspects, who all appeared nervous, except for Ms. LaFarge, who was giving him an appraising look. He made a point of making eye contact with each of them to see who among them would look away. All but one looked away, and that one, Ms. LaFarge, made him look away.

Grave sighed. "Coffee will be fine."

"Very good sir," said Smithers. "You'll find that, as well as an assortment of pastries and bagels, in the drawing room. From what I hear, they are to die for."

"Good to know, Smithers." He glanced around the foyer. "Now, before I begin, I have a question for all of you."

Eyes rolled in unison to the ceiling. "Don't worry, it's not hard. I just need a show of hands. If you're left-handed, raise your hand."

Everyone raised their hands. Impossible, thought Grave, and then another thought intruded.

"Ah, I see, I'm apparently talking with a British accent. Now, anyone who thinks I'm talking like a Brit, keep your hands raised."

Everyone kept their hands raised.

"Bloody hell," said Grave, immediately recognizing that he was, in fact, lapsing again.

"Okay, let's try this. First, put your hands down." Everyone complied.

"Now, don't do anything until I say go. If you're left-handed, raise your left hand and if you think I'm speaking with a British accent, raise your right hand. Okay, then, *go*."

Everyone raised their left hand and all but Smithers raised their right hand.

"So I'm not speaking with an accent, Smithers?"

"No, you are sir, but it's all a jumble this time. My language processors indicate an accent part British, part Australian, part South African, and part New Zealander. It's not unpleasant, though."

"Thank you, Smithers." He moved on to the more important result. "So, am I really to believe that each and every one of you is left-handed?"

Everyone nodded but Smithers, who raised both hands.

"The accent again, Smithers?"

"No sir, I'm ambidextrous."

Grave nodded. "Well, of course you are."

He sensed people had had enough of his unintended warmup exercise. "All right, then. *Mr. Hawthorne*, if you don't mind, we'll begin with you. And you, of course, Smithers."

He motioned Hawthorne toward the drawing room as the others quickly headed off to the temptations in the dining room. Hawthorne walked by him and headed for the room, his walk nothing like the flapping gait of Sergeant Blunt. He moved like a horse about to break into a gallop, knees lifted high, toes pointed to the floor with each step. Then again, if he had flapped his arms, he would have looked like a proud rooster.

Grave set these barnyard reflections aside, and followed Smithers and Hawthorne into the room.

13

The drawing room was clearly a room where you could withdraw from the world, or at least a world involving any of the last four or five centuries. Everything about the room suggested he was about to meet a French king named Louis, although Grave couldn't put his finger on the exact roman numeral designation for the king and the period furniture in the room.

The theme of the room was gilt without guilt. The arms and legs of all the uncomfortable chairs were gilt. The hundreds of paintings on the walls, all of red fish, featured ornately carved gilt frames. The wallpaper was pale blue with columns of golden fleur-de-lis from the floor to the ceiling, which was rimmed with equally ornate crown molding featuring gamboling golden cherubs. The upholstery featured golden threads, as did the carpets. And all of this glowed and glistered in the twinkling crystal light of a golden chandelier.

Grave and Hawthorne silently prepared their coffees, both ignoring the pastries and bagels on the sideboard, then sat down opposite each other and did their best to squirm into chairs apparently intended for people the size of children, each appraising the other as they swirled tiny gold spoons in their tiny gold-rimmed cups. Smithers stood at attention, and attentiveness, near the door.

Grave didn't know what Hawthorne made of him, although he sensed some disdain in the way the man's well-groomed, fluffy-caterpillar moustache twitched. What Grave saw in Hawthorne was a man who enjoyed playing the part of a new-tech entrepreneur, complete with sandals, jeans, and the ever-present black turtleneck.

Darius Hawthorne was a tall man, and suffered from the stoop that came when a boy grows faster than his peers, his extraordinary height problematic for all but his high school's basketball coach, prompting him to hunch over in a desperate attempt to seek eye level with his friends. Not that he would have played basketball, his awkwardness adding to his feelings that he was unworthy to walk among his fellow classmates. While other teenagers were forming garage bands and hanging out at malls, he had retreated to his garage to tinker on various electromechanical and digital devices, including prototypes for what Hawthorne dubbed "The Darion Simcortex," a patented device that had, through years of refinements, accelerated the evolution of robots, particularly their ability to mimic the functioning of the human brain, taking artificial intelligence to unheard of heights. At eighteen, he had formed a company that quickly became a juggernaut, Ramrod Robotics. The company's first products were vacuuming robots and a less successful product line of robotic lawnmowers, but it was the development of humanlike robots controlled by the now sophisticated Darion Simcortex that set the company apart from all others.

Hawthorne ran a finger around the rim of his turtleneck and lifted his head as if he were posing for the cover of *Fortune* magazine, which he had already done a half-dozen times. It was a face worthy of covers, a pleasingly proportioned assemblage of flesh and cartilage featuring bluer than blue eyes behind rimless glasses sitting on a nonintrusive nose, all made more arrogant by his slyly smiling mouth, which seemed to be moving now. At age forty-eight, his close-cropped brown hair already had traces of gray at the temples. In short, if "arrogance" was a soccer team, he would have been its goalie, haughtily brushing aside ball after ball.

"Shall we get on with it, then?" he said, setting down his cup on the gilt and glass table between them, his hands shaking just enough to rattle the cup on the saucer. He quickly folded his hands in front of him to stem the shaking. Grave couldn't tell whether the man was nervous or angry.

Grave, in turn, set down his cup, casually unbuttoned his suit jacket, slowly pulled out Blunt's notes, which he hadn't had time to read, clicked open his pen, and began, or at least tried to begin, Hawthorne taking advantage of the pause to jump in with his own agenda.

"I assume you are here to discuss the missing trophy," he said. "The MacGuffin."

"Hardly," said Grave. "In case you missed it, a young woman was murdered in your mansion night before last."

Hawthorne looked exasperated. "Now see here, even a cretin would know that people locked in a room that can only be locked from the *outside* could not possibly have committed that murder. How could we get out? There's only the one door, and the windows don't open. And how could we possibly lock ourselves in? I mean, surely you see my point."

Grave couldn't deny the logic, but he had long ago learned to follow his gut and not that wormy looking gray mass between his ears. Besides, Hawthorne's logic was incomplete.

"Well, one might ask how an inanimate object, this trophy of yours, managed to steal itself, leave the room, and lock you in."

Hawthorne frowned. "That again. Well, it's puzzling, I'll grant you that."

Grave knew that Hawthorne was obsessed with the trophy, and seemed to care very little about Ms. Jones, so he decided to take down the basic facts as a way to getting to the murder.

"Very well, tell me about this MacGuffin Trophy."

Hawthorne launched into a description of the trophy and its import to his world. Like many sports trophies, it had been created long ago, in the age of craftsmanship, when trophies were rightly considered works of art for their form and line and intricate engraving. What set the MacGuffin apart, apparently, were the hundreds of blue sapphires that formed a simulated rolling sea atop the foot-tall trophy, with a solid gold, lost-wax sculpture of a sailing ship coursing at full sail. In artistic terms, it was priceless. In monetary terms, it was valued well in excess of ten million dollars.

Grave couldn't help whistling appreciatively when he heard this. "I understand your concern now. I thought the trophy was one of those nice looking but cheap affairs you might buy at Uncle Bob's Trophy Shop." Grave actually had one, a trophy with a crab on top, swinging a baseball bat, recognition for his participation as first baseman for the Crab Cove Claws, his youth baseball team.

Hawthorne winced at that analogy, but seemed somewhat relieved. "Definitely an upgrade from that. So you see my situation. As the winner of last year's race, I was entrusted with this trophy, and if I can't find it, I'm not only on the hook for its replacement value—not that it can be replaced—but I'm likely to be expelled from the yacht club. I simply couldn't bear that."

Grave doubted Hawthorne would have to pay a dime. Surely, there would be a suitably massive insurance policy. What he did wonder was why the yacht club would let the trophy out of its sight for even a minute. Then again, the wealthy were a curious lot.

"Here's what I'll do," said Grave. "My interest, of course, is homicide, but logic certainly suggests there may be a connection between the trophy and the murder. Find the trophy, find the murderer, if you see what I mean."

Hawthorne nodded. "Of course. And that murderer is out there somewhere—not here—doing who knows what with my trophy."

"Or perhaps the trophy is still here, somewhere in this massive mansion. I presume we may search high and low for it here?"

Hawthorne nodded, clearly with some reluctance.

Grave leaned forward. "I promise you we'll pursue this with the same vigor we'll use to investigate the murder. In fact, henceforth, I'll refer to this case as The MacGuffin Murder."

Hawthorne was clearly relieved. "Thank you, detective." He stood as if to go.

"No, no," said Grave. "Please sit down. We still have to talk about the murder of young Ms. Jones."

Hawthorne slumped back down into the chair, which emitted a squeak worthy of a French king.

"This won't take long, I assure you," said Grave, although he had every intention of asking an exhaustive series of questions designed to learn more about the other suspects and Hawthorne himself.

Hawthorne nodded his grudging acquiescence, and Grave began, almost immediately interrupted by a strange whirring sound coming from Smithers, who slapped at himself as if trying to stifle a gurgling stomach.

"Sorry, sir," he said. "Lube cycle in progress."

14

Hawthorne was more cooperative than Grave expected, and was more than willing to comment on any topic, sometimes at great length and in more detail than necessary.

Hawthorne had moved into the mansion just two years previously, at the insistence of its owner, his new second wife, Philomena, who abhorred his large, one-room loft atop the Ramrod Robotics manufacturing plant, and wanted something grander, away from the bustle and noise of the factory. The two had met shortly after the death of his first wife, who had fallen from a catwalk above the plant floor. They married just six months later.

The mansion was so big, so massive, the newlyweds had invited Hawthorne's children, Whitney and wheelchair-bound Edwina, and Whitney's son, Roy Lynn, to move in with them. Whitney had balked at first, but when she learned about the studio, she was sold. Edwina really had no choice in the matter, and was brought to the mansion as a cost-saving measure. In the bargain, she got a full-time nurse to help her through the day. They had then hired Lola LaFarge to serve that role, with the additional duty of home schooling and civilizing the near feral Roy Lynn.

From Hawthorne's point of view, everyone got along with everyone, except for Roy Lynn, whose manner, demeanor, and behavior was well beyond rapscallion and just past incorrigible on the juvenile delinquent scale. Even so, their lives seemed almost charmed, at least until the disappearance of the MacGuffin Trophy.

"And, of course, the unfortunate murder of Ms. Jones," Hawthorne quickly added.

"Tell me about your relationship with Ms. Jones," Grave said, notebook and pen at the ready.

Hawthorne squirmed in his seat. "Not much to tell, really. You should really ask Whitney about her. I saw her only occasionally, and always briefly, when she stopped by to pick up more paintings to sell, or to talk privately with Whitney."

"You do know they were lovers."

Hawthorne looked away briefly, then turned back. "Yes, everyone knew. There aren't too many secrets in this house, and I couldn't care less, really, about my children's sex lives, or in Edwina's case, the lack thereof."

Grave made a quick note about Edwina. He wondered whether that was true. "Whitney's divorced, correct?"

"Oh, no. Her husband, Churn N. Waters, died in Afghanistan a few years back, or at least went missing. The troop carrier he was riding in hit one of those homemade mines. Everyone died, but Churn was never found. Probably blown to bits is my guess. Anyway, Whitney had always leaned more toward women, so when Ms. Jones came along, eager to advance Whitney's career, she advanced on other fronts as well."

Grave pressed on. "When was the last time you saw Ms. Jones?"

Hawthorne didn't hesitate. "A week ago. I had been working in my basement laboratory and heard a ruckus coming from the foyer. When I arrived there, Whitney and Piph—er, Ms. Jones—were tugging at a painting, both of them screaming for the other to let go. I intervened, of course, and Ms. Jones turned on her heels and left—without the painting."

"And what caused this tiff with Piph?"

Hawthorne laughed. "Oh, it was much more than just a tiff. Unkind words were exchanged, middle fingers were raised. Whitney shouted that she should never come back."

"Never come back? But why then was she invited back for the unveiling of the new painting, the trophy painting?"

Hawthorne shrugged. "I have no idea. All I can say is that Whitney was insistent that we wait for Ms. Jones to show up before she would unveil the painting. They must have made up sometime during the week."

Grave made a few notes, wondering whether make-up sex was involved. He suppressed the thought and the obvious imagery that sprang to mind. "Let's move on."

"Certainly," said Hawthorne. "What would you like to know?"

Grave looked over at Smithers. "Smithers, could you come over here, please?"

Smithers walked over, and Grave motioned him into the chair next to Hawthorne.

"I can't tell you how much I've enjoyed meeting your Smithers. I love that you've given him a voice like Richard Burton's, but he doesn't look like Burton. I think he looks like an actor, but I can't quite put my finger on it."

Hawthorne smiled. "It's Peter O'Toole you're thinking of, one of my favorite actors, and as for his voice, yes, it's Burton's. But not just *like* Burton's. It is Burton's voice. During his career, Burton said about every word in the dictionary, so it was relatively easy, at least technically, to create a database of Burton's own words for Smithers to access. There are still some rough spots—problems with inflection and word linkages, for example—but on the whole, Smithers can deliver a coherent and smooth onslaught of words in Burton's voice."

"I understand the voice, but why not make Smithers look like Burton as well?"

"Ah, just personal preference, really. Burton's appeal was all about his wonderful voice. He was handsome, true, but his face was just not as expressive as I wanted. Now, Peter O'Toole, on the other hand, could put a complete novel of emotion into the slight twitch of his brows, and his eyes could just penetrate you."

"Yes, I can see that." He looked at Smithers, who was working his way through his program, showing off the many ways his brows could twitch and arch.

"That's enough, Smithers," said Hawthorne, tapping Smithers on the shoulder, the robot immediately complying, his eyebrows dropping to their default position: quizzical delight.

"Fascinating," said Grave, truly impressed. "I'd really like to learn a bit more about robots, Mr. Hawthorne."

Hawthorne brightened even more. "They are my passion, detective. What would you like to know?"

"As I understand it, Ashcroft's Law prevents robots from harming humans."

Hawthorne laughed. "Ha! I get this all the time, and it's Asimov's Law, by the way, the much talked about Three Laws of Robotics. Did you know Asimov proposed a fourth law, which he called the zeroth law? That one's do no harm to humanity itself, and it's all fiction, I'm afraid."

"Fiction?"

"Yes. Smithers here makes no distinction between humans and robots. He sees and categorizes shapes, with high precision, mind, but to be clear, he knows your shape and the way you move and speak is you, even your lapses into a somewhat British accent, but he does not classify you as either human or robot. You are simply a collection of data points identified as Detective Grave."

"So he could, in fact, harm humans."

Hawthorne shook his head. "If he did, it would be purely accidental. He is programmed to carry out certain functions, based on programmed commands, and nothing more. Butler programming, if you will, and a few other tasks."

"But he *could* harm someone," said Grave. "I mean, in a butlerish way, as he carried out his duties."

"No, you're not following me. I'm not a detective, detective, and I don't play one on TV, but I have watched a ton of mysteries, and they always, or nearly always, talk about motive, means, and opportunity."

"Yes, that's right."

"Well, let's say Smithers here is in the kitchen with Ms. Jones, and there's a knife handy on the counter, the *means*. Yes, he would have the *opportunity* to kill her, but he lacks *motive*. And he lacks motive because there is nothing in his program that would suggest that he should insert a knife into her back. He lacks emotions, you see."

"Wait, you just said he had a full range of emotions."

"No, detective, Smithers here has a full range of *expressions*, responses to emotion, tone of voice, and textual content and context he detects in others. If you call for help, he will express alarm and act accordingly, but his actions are never prompted by emotions."

Grave tried his best to digest this. "I see, but what if Ms. Jones provoked him in some way. Maybe slapped him, or something?"

"He would attempt to stay on task. If she slapped him again, he would ask for a new instruction. It's all programming, and it's quite extensive. We cover the gamut of possibilities."

"Okay, I understand that, but bear with me. What if someone instructed Smithers to stab Ms. Jones?"

"Wouldn't work. There is simply nothing in his program involving slicing into an object with that shape, in this case, Ms. Jones."

"I see."

"I hope so," said Hawthorne. "Robots have not quite progressed to the levels forecast by science fiction. We're getting there, but for now, it's not robots humanity has to worry about—it's humanity itself."

Grave slumped back in his chair, reflecting on what he had just heard.

Hawthorne glanced at his watch, sweeping it up in front of his face with a flourish befitting a Rolex. "Will that be all, detective? I really have to see to the other robots."

Grave snapped out of it. "What? There are *more* robots?"

"Why, yes. You don't think Smithers could handle all that's entailed with the upkeep of this mansion, do you?"

"But how many robots, and where are they?"

"Ah, I see your point. When you arrived the other evening, all of us were locked in the studio with Smithers, and the other robots, ten in all, were in the laboratory below, nestled safely into their recharging units, something we do every Friday." He chuckled. "It's sort of like giving the servants the night off."

"So they could have locked you in."

"No, that's impossible. Once they hook up for the recharge, they are there for the length of the charge, and wouldn't self-activate again until the following afternoon. And I had checked them all before going to the studio. They were all plugged in, isn't that right, Smithers?"

"Yes, sir," said Smithers. He really did look like Peter O'Toole.

"Wait, Smithers was with you?"

"Yes, he's a little more than a butler, you see. Assists me in the lab from time to time. Hand me this, hand me that, and so forth."

"And why wasn't Smithers charging along with the others?"

"Normally, he would have been, but the event in the studio, you see. We needed someone to handle the champagne."

"I see. Tell me, could someone have activated the other robots before they had fully recharged?"

"Yes, it's possible, but again, robots aren't programmed to kill people. They just aren't. And for what it's worth, there's nothing to indicate their charge was interrupted. They all reactivated at 2:00 p.m. precisely, as scheduled, fully charged."

"I see."

"So, can I go now?"

"One last question, if you don't mind. This charging business. Do the robots behave normally when their batteries are low, or is it just a case of they're working, and then they're not?"

"They do slow down a bit, but that typically happens just seconds before the end of their charge. Speech becomes slurred and so on. All the things you'd expect from a fading battery. But again, only for a few seconds."

Grave was struggling with just how to form the next question. He kept running into words that suggested an intelligence—a humanness—that was beyond a robot's capacity, at least if Hawthorne was to be believed. He finally gave up and asked the question. "What about their judgment, their decision-making abilities? In short, is there any reason to suspect that they might abandon their programming or their protocols when their batteries are running low?"

Grave could see the answer in Hawthorne's smirk. "No, detective, they just slow down a bit, like a defensive football player who's been on the field too long."

"I see."

Hawthorne checked his Rolex again. "Detective, please, may I go now?"

"One last question."

"I thought you already asked your last question."

"Oh, that was the next to last question."

"All right, then, what?"

"I haven't noticed any security cameras. Do you have any, and if so, where?"

Hawthorne shook his head. "No, not a one. Never felt the need. Any important work I do is done at Ramrod Robotics, not here."

"What about a basic security system?"

"That's yet another question, but no again. We had one installed when we first moved in, but it was such a nuisance, going off all times of the night in this drafty old mansion, we disarmed it."

"I see."

"*Now* can I go?"

Grave nodded. "Yes, of course, and would you send in Whitney for me?"

Hawthorne gave a quick nod and headed for the door. Grave called out to him just as he reached it.

"Think fast," he shouted, tossing the old tennis ball in the air toward Hawthorne, who snatched it out of the air with his right hand.

Grave smiled. "So, you're *not* left handed, after all."

Hawthorne tossed the ball back to Grave using his left hand.

"Actually, detective, I think you'll find that left-handed ball players catch with a glove on their *right* hand."

"Yes, of course they do," said Grave, stuffing the ball quickly into his pocket. "Bollocks!"

Hawthorne and Smithers raised their hands.

15

Grave took advantage of the time between interviews to read Blunt's notes from the previous day. He had apparently disappeared behind his cloak of invisibility shortly after entering the studio. No one had paid him the least mind, and had talked as if he weren't there. Most of the conversations had been focused on the absurdity of treating them as suspects, and their pressing need to use the bathroom, which had several of them dancing in place. It had been a great relief to all, so to speak, when he had received Grave's orders to escort them to the bathroom one by one. And it had been an even greater relief to Blunt when Smithers took over the task.

He glanced at the door. Whitney had yet to appear.

"Smithers, could you see what's keeping Ms. Waters?"

Smithers stood. "Of course, sir. I'll be but a moment." He walked to the door in a way that suggested supreme confidence, even arrogance. Grave couldn't help but wonder if Hawthorne ever dressed him up as Lawrence of Arabia.

Grave pulled out his cellphone and called Blunt, who picked up after one ring.

"Blunt here."

"Anything yet?" said Grave.

"Yes, it seems that the oil, the proto oil, has a variety of uses, but its most important application is in robotics."

"Interesting. Any connection with Ramrod Robotics?"

"Yes, in fact, they're the major user in the entire area—buy it in fifty-gallon drums."

"Well, that's certainly a link. What about robotics parts or tools? Anything resembling an icepick?"

There was a moment of silence on the line. Grave could hear papers being shuffled, and then Blunt was back on the line.

"Nothing yet, and I doubt there will be. Ramrod, it seems, manufactures most of their own parts. The parts deliveries I've found are exclusively for replacement parts to precision lathes, metal molding machines, and those new 3-D printers. Nothing at all like an icepick, I'm afraid."

"I guess that makes sense. Corporate secrets and all that."

"Yes, sir."

"All right, then. Put that aside for now. The interviews here are going more slowly than I'd hoped, so I could use you here. Believe it or not, Hawthorne has ten more robots roaming around the mansion. I haven't seen any of them yet, but I'd like you to check them out when you arrive."

"Will do, sir."

Grave ended the call and sat for some moments in silence, trying his best to piece together the puzzle parts, but knew that like any investigation in its early stages, he didn't have all the pieces, and the pieces he did have were changing shape by the minute. Fortunately, the door creaked open, and Whitney walked into the room carrying a painting under her arm, followed at a deferent, butlerly distance by Smithers, who carefully closed the door behind him and resumed his tape-recorder position against the wall.

Whitney strode across the room, shaking a finger at him and struggling to find just the right expletive to use in her spitting-mad opening salvo.

Grave clenched the arms of the chair and prepared to receive.

16

Whitney's emotions seemed to be activated and deactivated by a simple on-off switch in her brain that could take her from rage to supreme calm in an instant. The moment she had finished with her arms-on-hips opening salvo—the absurdity of being treated as a suspect, the outrage that she could not be left to grieve, the further outrage that she would be interviewed at all, and the lack of respect for her feelings in general—she grew calm and sat down across from Grave, the painting face down in her lap as if it was some sort of surprise that she was not yet ready to reveal.

Whether raging or at rest, she was a beautiful woman, although not in the classical cover girl sense. She was moon faced and freckled, with emerald green eyes and Godiva-length red hair. Her neck was long and smooth, her skin, freckled as it was, like alabaster. When she spoke, the right side of her mouth curled up higher than the left side, which gave every word a sensual, sexual import far beyond the words themselves. She could have been reading the Gettysburg address, and you would have thought she was flirting with you, her voice, deep and sexy, amplifying the effect.

The wondrous body that she had displayed on their first meeting was now clothed simply in a pullover gray jersey and torn jeans, although she remained barefoot, each toenail painted the same red as all her paintings, with a little silver toe ring on the big toe of her right foot, which bobbed up and down suggestively as she sat there with her legs crossed, smiling at him. In short, if "sexy" was a baseball team, she would have been the player who hit it out of the park.

"Ms. Waters, I know you are upset," he began, "and rightly so, but I have a few questions I must ask. And understand, if we are to catch the murderer, I need your fullest cooperation. Every detail, however small, may be important."

Whitney dropped the smile and leveled her gaze on him. "Just understand from the get-go, Mr. Detective, I did not kill Piph." She said the last few words as if a full-stop period followed each.

"We'll begin with that assumption, then," he said. "Tell me about your relationship with Ms. Jones."

Through tears, which may or may not have been heartfelt—Grave didn't know her well enough to tell for sure—she recounted their first meeting, their rather straightforward artist-broker business arrangement, and that special evening when they shared a bottle of wine after a recent sale and one thing led to another.

The relationship had gone well for many months, but then the economy had turned like the worm it often is, and sales plummeted. As Whitney continued to paint, the paintings themselves overwhelmed Piph's small retail gallery, forcing her to stack them in the backroom, until even that overflowed. Whitney was forced to stockpile them in the mansion, and as big as the mansion was, even she was running out of walls and storage areas.

"As I understand it," said Grave, "the two of you argued heatedly over a painting just a week ago."

Whitney nodded, then shook her head. "Yes, no—well, yes, I guess so. She didn't want to take the painting, which hurt my feelings. I exploded on her, which hurt *her* feelings, and so it was basically the two of us pushing the painting back and forth, each wanting the other to take it. In the end, it became absurd, and we ended up laughing it off."

"Really? I heard that harsh words, and gestures, were exchanged."

"Just words, detective." She waved a hand in the air dismissively.

"So there was no animosity between the two of you?"

"No, not at all. We were just letting off steam, and we were still very much in love."

"Do you know anyone who would *want* to kill Ms. Jones?"

"I've been thinking of little else, detective." She shook her head.

"But I can't think of anyone here who would do her harm, not even Philomena."

"Mr. Hawthorne's wife, your stepmother."

She visibly winced at *stepmother*. "Yes, she's a piece of work, that woman—hates us all, I think—but I can't see her hurting anyone physically. She kills with looks, if you know what I mean."

"No, what do you mean?"

Whitney gave him a smirk. "Let's just say it was dad's idea to let us all stay here. Philomena was against the whole idea, and nothing would make her happier than seeing us gone."

"I see," said Grave, making a quick note and then pressing on. "Do you know anyone who would want you to take the blame for the murder?"

She seemed genuinely surprised. "Why, no, of course not. Why would you ask that?"

Grave told her about the three obvious clues from the body: the rose, the arrow, and the happy face.

"I would never, Roy Lynn would never," she began. "It's just, just *absurd*." The import of the clues then took hold. "Oh, my god, who would do that to me?"

"That's what I aim to find out," said Grave. "And do you see any significance to the rose? Was she into flamenco dancing?"

"I really have no idea," she said, "but we do have roses in the gardens. You should ask dad or our gardener, Jimmy."

Grave made a few notes and moved on.

"So, when I left your studio on Saturday, was there any discussion?"

"Yes, we were all annoyed that you would even think to detain us, or suspect us of anything criminal."

"Nothing else?"

Whitney blanched, even her freckles appearing to fade a shade or two. "Again, nothing to be concerned about, at least for your investigation. Dad was *confused* by how I had done the painting, and said as much." She lifted the painting on her lap and turned it face out to Grave.

"A fish?" said Grave. "Why would he be upset about a fish? All the paintings I've seen so far have been of the same fish."

Whitney shook her head in a way that only an artist would shake her head when she's dealing with a non-artist's interpretation of her paintings. "You see a fish, Dad sees a fish, when it's quite obvious that the fish represents the very essence of the MacGuffin Trophy."

Grave stared at the painting again, then at all the other identical paintings on the walls of the drawing room, and tried his best to transform the red fish he saw into a priceless, bejeweled trophy topped with a sailing ship.

"Okay," he said, drawing the word out like taffy.

Whitney gave out an exasperated sigh and began pointing at various parts of the red fish. "Look, here is the trophy's base, here its handles, here the proud sailing ship—it's just so *obvious*."

"I guess so," he said, unconvinced.

"Detective, I'm surprised—no, *shocked*—that you, a detective would not understand that the whole purpose of a red herring is to make people think it's something else."

Grave gathered himself to make a couple of points he knew would not be received well. "What you say is true, as far as it goes, because first, a red herring is not what it purports to be, but what it is in actuality, in this case a smoked fish of a red color. And second, that is not a painting of a red herring."

"What?" Whitney looked at the painting, then back at Grave. "What do you mean it isn't a red herring? Of course it is."

"Hand me the painting, and I'll explain."

She handed it over, then flung herself back in her chair with her arms crossed. She was not going down without a fight. "Show me, then."

He set the painting in his lap, the fish facing Whitney, and pointed at the fish's dorsal fins. "Here is where you made your error, Ms. Waters. You have a fish with two dorsal fins, here and here, and then a long line of dorsal finlets running down the spine to the rear."

She nodded. "Yes, of course I do. They're very expressive, don't you think? In fact, if you look closely at my paintings, you'll find those fins to be highly nuanced, each to symbolize different aspects of the human experience, and in the case of this particular painting, the very trophy itself."

It was the kind of artsy-fartsy description you would find in any artist's catalog. Grave let her have her moment of vainglorious glory, but then put her into her misery. "The problem, I'm afraid, is that a herring only has one dorsal fin, with no finlets."

She sat bolt upright. "What? Are you sure?"

"Quite sure. You can google it if you don't believe me."

Whitney stared back at him blankly, then at the painting on his lap, then at all the paintings on the walls, trying to absorb what she had just heard. "Well, if it's not a herring, what is it?"

"A mackerel, I'm afraid."

Whitney was clearly crushed and appeared to crumple into tears in the way any artist would crumple when faced with the realization that their entire career had been based on a mackerel, and not a holy one at that.

17

Grave had been willing to give Ms. Waters a mulligan on her obvious mistake, creating a painting of a MacGuffin in the guise of a red herring, when it was in reality a red mackerel, completely distorting any resemblance to the hallowed trophy, but she had been inconsolable and had rushed from the room, tearing her painting to shreds as she left, the door slamming hard behind her.

Smithers walked over to Grave, who was trying to collect himself in the wake of her abrupt departure. "I so enjoy Ms. Waters. Her range of expressions is quite extraordinary."

"Yes, she's quite beside herself."

Smithers adjusted his face to suggest *quizzical*. "I saw only one Ms. Waters. Did you see two?"

Grave was puzzled at first, but then latched on to the meaning of what Smithers was saying. "Oh, that was just an idiom, a way of saying she was very upset."

"I see," said Smithers with a little shrug. "I will add that to my idiom databank."

Grave had an idea. "Smithers, can I ask you a question?"

"Yes, of course."

"Do you see yourself as a robot or a human?"

Smithers whirred for some seconds, his eyebrows squirming as he searched for an answer in his programming.

"I found the definitions, sir, but neither seems to fit my perception of what I am."

"How so?"

"One seems too low an estimation, and the other seems too high. If I had to describe myself, I would say I was a bipedal mobile device with sensory and electromechanical capabilities."

"And how would you describe Ms. Waters?"

Smithers didn't hesitate. "The same way, but I'd have to say she's more expressive than I am."

"And when you said you *enjoy* Ms. Waters, what did you mean?"

"Ah," said Smithers. "You want to know if I feel emotions."

"Yes, precisely."

"The answer is a bit complex, but the upshot is no, I feel nothing."

"So enjoy is—?"

"A summation, more or less, of the number of definitions I must access to determine what is happening around me and how I should then respond. The more definitions accessed, the more *enjoyment*."

"But the enjoyment, as you put it, doesn't make you smile?"

Smithers seemed puzzled. "No, should it?"

"No, I guess not," said Grave. "Let's move on, if you don't mind. I'd like to interview Edwina. Could you bring her here, please?"

"Certainly." Smithers turned and walked from the room, leaving Grave to reflect on the interview with Whitney, Edwina's twin sister. He wasn't sure he bought her explanations of the arguments she had had with Ms. Jones or her father. She was holding back something, or at least that's what the bipedal mobile device that was Detective Grave had perceived. But he was *enjoying* the fact that he was working on a case that no longer involved hundreds of red herrings, not that there weren't a few.

18

Echoes are funny things. Done well, they resound as if from every direction. Done in a massive mansion of marble and gilt, however, the echoes have the effect of self-locating, particularly when obscenities are involved. So it was that when Lola LaFarge pushed open the door to the drawing room and rolled wheelchair-bound Edwina in, the echoes of Whitney's shrill concatenation of every obscenity known to man, and perhaps robot, came rushing from her studio, whooshing down the staircase and into the drawing room, reverberating endlessly until Ms. LaFarge quickly closed the door and uttered one word, "Bitch."

The room grew comfortably quiet, save for the noticeable squeak coming from the left wheel of Edwina's wheelchair. Ms. LaFarge pushed aside the interview chair and rolled Edwina to a stop across from him.

Save for her hair, which had been buzz cut to near baldness, Edwina was the very image of Whitney, each freckle seemingly locked in place like stars in the night sky. The lack of hair had the effect of making her green eyes appear larger than Whitney's, but not to the point of suggesting the preternaturally large eyes in a painting by Keane. Her body, at least from the waist up, was just as glorious as Whitney's. The rest of her was hidden beneath a blanket with a tartan pattern, which if he had to guess, was for members of Clan MacDonald and its septs, which he suspected included Hawthorne, a crosshatch of red lines creating not unpleasant squares of various hues of green and blue. His knowledge of all things clans came from a previous case, in which the killer mistakenly used a Stewart tartan instead of a Campbell tartan, the "AND" he had tried to explain to Polk.

Edwina stared at him as if she were looking past him to some distant void in the universe. In short, if "awareness" was a motel, hers would have been flashing a vacancy sign.

He attempted to make contact. "Good morning, Ms. Hawthorne."

Nothing.

"I'm afraid she's not that talkative," said Ms. LaFarge.

"I see," said Grave. He suppressed the impulse to wave a hand in front of Edwina's face to see if anyone was at home. There clearly wasn't. "Has she always been this way?"

"Well, since I've known her. Apparently, she saw something that greatly upset her—I have no idea what—and just shut down."

"Completely?"

"Mostly. She can chew and swallow and do everything else related to processing food, often without warning, but she doesn't speak or walk or use her hands, except for an occasional involuntary twitch. I've tried getting her to blink for yes and no, but even that doesn't work. She's pretty much a vegetable on wheels."

Grave frowned at Ms. LaFarge, surprised by her insensitive comment.

"Don't give me that look, detective," she said. "I'm the one who has to lift her and wash her and take care of her every need."

"I didn't mean to suggest—"

She sighed, frustrated. "Sorry, but sometimes all *this* just gets to me."

"I understand, I really do." Grave sat back in his chair and considered what to do next. He hadn't expected Edwina to be this unresponsive. Hadn't she raised her hands in the left-handedness exercise? He felt sure she had, but with so many hands in the air, perhaps he was mistaken. At any rate, given this harsh news, Edwina was clearly not a suspect. Even so, it was important to place her whereabouts before and after entering the studio on Friday night. "You'll have to be her voice, then."

"Okay, what do you want to know?"

"How did the two of you get to the studio that night?"

"Pretty straightforward, really. I left my bedroom at about 7:45, went to hers, got her out of bed, made her presentable, and pushed her down the hall to the studio. We were a little late, maybe ten minutes or so."

"And did you see anyone else along the way?"

Ms. LaFarge briefly looked at the ceiling, which in Grave's experience was a common posture for people trying to recall past events. In fact, he was always suspicious of people who *didn't* look at the ceiling and just came straight out with information, as if they had practiced it over and over.

"No, not a single soul, but . . ." Her voice trailed off.

"Yes?"

"It's probably nothing, but I thought I heard a thwacking sound coming from the foyer."

"Thwacking?"

"Or squelching. Really, it's hard to describe. It was like the hitting sound made by one of those damned arrows with the suction cups that Roy Lynn shoots every which way. Of course, it couldn't have been him. He was with us, and I was watching him like a hawk."

"Did others arrive after you?"

She paused briefly, then shook her head. "No, we were the last three to arrive."

Grave suddenly realized that Smithers, his erstwhile tape recorder, was not in the room. "Damn!"

"What?"

"Not you. Smithers has gone missing." He started to go on, then changed his mind. "I wonder, would you mind popping outside to see if you can find Smithers. I'm using him to record my interviews, so . . ."

Ms. LaFarge shrugged. "Not at all. Be back in a moment."

She walked across the room and slipped out. Whitney's screams

A Grave Misunderstanding

had apparently abated, but in the brief few seconds that the door was open, Grave was sure he saw fish paintings sailing past the door like Frisbees.

Grave waited until the door clicked shut behind Ms. LaFarge to unleash his frustration. "Bloody, bloody hell!"

Edwina raised her arm above her head. There seemed to be a mischievous gleam in her eyes.

80

19

The few minutes between the departure of Ms. LaFarge and her return with a seemingly reluctant Smithers had been exhilarating. Not only could Edwina raise her hands, but under the influence of his most arch British accent, she could answer simple yes-no questions by blinking her eyes, once for yes, twice for no. Given enough time, he thought he might be able to even raise her from her wheelchair. As it was, he was only able to ascertain that Ms. LaFarge's account of Friday evening was correct, at least so far.

"Here he is," said Ms. LaFarge, returning to her position behind Edwina's wheelchair.

"Thank you," Grave said, turning to Smithers. "Where were you?"

Smithers gave a little shrug. "I was with Mr. Hawthorne, trying to calm Ms. Waters." He emitted a whirring sound. "Unsuccessfully, I'm afraid."

"I'll let you get back to that in a few minutes, once I finish questioning Ms. Hawthorne."

"But she—" Smithers began.

"I know," said Grave, cutting him off. "Ms. LaFarge here is actually answering the questions."

"Very good, sir." Smithers resumed his position near the door and recorded in silence.

Grave turned to Ms. LaFarge. "Okay, you took Edwina into Whitney's studio. What happened next?"

Ms. LaFarge looked briefly at the ceiling, finding her place. "I positioned her along the side wall of the studio, where she could see the unveiling without getting in the way."

Grave gave Edwina a quick glance, hoping for some hint of affirmation, but she was back in her nonresponsive mode. "And you stayed with her?"

"Um, at first, but after a few minutes, I left her to get a glass of champagne. It had been a long day."

"I see, and after that?"

"She didn't really need me, so I mingled with the others as we waited for the arrival of Ms. Jones, and we all know how that turned out."

"And how many glasses of champagne did you have?"

Ms. LaFarge gave him a surprised look. "Is that really relevant?"

"Perhaps. How many?"

"Three," she said resignedly. "No, four."

"Why so much?"

She resented him pressing her further on this topic. "As I *said*, it had been a long day. It was Friday, after all, and I was going to have the next day off, or at least I *thought* I was, so . . ."

"I see," said Grave. "Now, when exactly did everyone realize they were locked in the room?"

"About half an hour later, say 8:40 or so, I think. Whitney had grown impatient and had set out to see if Ms. Jones was anywhere in the mansion."

"Couldn't she have just called her?"

Ms. LaFarge gave her head a little shake and gave him a scolding look. "Detective, you seem to have forgotten that no one had a cell phone."

"And why exactly was that?"

"Whitney is a phonophobe, if that's the right term. It was a stipulation of attendance. She didn't want anything to interrupt the ceremony she had planned. And we all apparently complied."

"So Whitney was the first to try the door?"

"Yes, and then me, and then Smithers, I think. Not Roy Lynn, though, or Mr. and Mrs. Hawthorne. Philomena knew it was locked, or at least knew there was no hope of opening the door from inside the room."

He had one final question for her. "And from the best of your recollection, everyone was in that room the whole time, from the moment you entered to the moment you left?"

Ms. LaFarge seemed puzzled. "Well, duh, of course they were. There's only one door, and it was locked."

"But you'd had four glasses of champagne."

"Which can do nothing to help people walk through walls, detective."

He nodded curtly. "So it seems."

He glanced down at Edwina, whose left eye was twitching.

20

Grave sat alone in the drawing room, nibbling on a bagel that had managed to go stale during the morning's interviews. Ms. LaFarge and Edwina were long gone, and he had sent Smithers in search of Sergeant Blunt, who was probably somewhere in the house with the other robots.

Grave had two conflicting thoughts on what to do next, both offering exciting possibilities. First, his success in rousing Edwina back into awareness could be the key to the whole mystery. He needed to get her alone somehow, away from Ms. LaFarge, and grill her on what actually took place in that locked studio. Second, and perhaps most tantalizing, he wanted to bolt from the mansion, drive to his therapist's office, and boast about the new-found advantages of the British accent she had been trying to wrest from his being these many months.

Both thoughts danced in his head, going from a simple two-step, to a waltz, to the twist, to the mashed potato, to the pony, to the spastic and maniacal moves he himself would invent on the dancefloor after a few glasses of wine, the safety of his partner's feet be damned.

There was a knock at the door, Blunt's signature warning tap that he was about to enter the room with or without permission, the door swinging open seconds later, the blur that was Blunt entering quietly and closing the door behind him.

"Sir," he said curtly, in a way that suggested he was present and awaiting instructions or formulating a question, but not in a way that would suggest he had a specific question, and certainly not in a way that would require a question mark.

Grave ushered him to the chair opposite him, if only to keep him in one place. "A lot has happened."

"Sir," Blunt said, in a way that suggested he was ready to receive any and all information that Grave might care to share with him.

Grave shook his head. "We'll get to that later. Now, have you managed to see the other robots?"

"Yes, sir, and if I may say so, it's a bit disconcerting."

"What?"

"The robots, sir. Except for their voices and clothing, they're all the same. It's Smithers times ten, sir. You really need to see them. It's quite astonishing, really."

Grave tried his best to process the prospect of dealing with eleven Smithers, or Smitherses. "Blunt, I really don't have time to chase down ten robots today, particularly if they all look alike. I still have to interview Mrs. Hawthorne, and—"

Blunt held up a hand, or at least a blur that might have been a hand. "They're right outside, sir, in the foyer, awaiting your inspection."

"I see. Well, then, lead on." He stood and walked with Blunt out into the foyer, which was now miraculously free of the flotsam and jetsam of Whitney's mackerel paintings. He came to an abrupt stop as he caught sight of the ten, no eleven, robots lined up to greet him, as if he were the lord of the manor returning home after a long absence, perhaps from a war of some kind, which had left him broken but still quite rich. He briefly imagined being greeted by the lady of the manor, or a friend of the lady of the manor, or just some woman, who would be dressed in riding clothes, complete with riding crop, jodhpurs, tall black boots, and riding helmet, because there was always such a woman, at least on Masterpiece Theater. Sometimes there would even be a horse.

"Disconcerting, indeed," he whispered in the general direction of Blunt, who had completely vanished.

He marched down the line of robots, pausing briefly to say hello, each responding in a different voice: James Earl Jones, Morgan

Freeman, Jeffrey Holder, Jack Nicholson, Jimmy Stewart, Clark Gable, Humphrey Bogart, Jimmy Cagney, John Wayne, Richard Burton, and perhaps most disconcerting, Marilyn Monroe, who was dressed in a copy of that "uplifting" signature white dress made famous in *The Seven Year Itch*.

Smithers stepped out of the line to offer his assistance. "Like me, sir, each performs a specific function." He walked down the line of Peter O'Toole lookalikes, tapping each on the shoulder as he went: "Cook, cook's assistant, gardener, chauffeur, downstairs maid, pool boy, horse trainer, stable boy, upstairs maid, and of course, our housekeeper, Marilyn."

Grave gave them all a blank look. Their clothing helped identify what they did, of course, but he was still not sure he would be able to keep track of them. He turned to Smithers. "Is their voice and clothing the only difference, then?"

Smithers looked confused at first, then pointed at his nametag, a small rectangular piece of gray plastic with "SMITHERS" engraved on it in all caps and "Butler" engraved on a line just below, in smaller type. Why hadn't he noticed this before?

"Oh," said Grave. "I see." He glanced at the closest robot other than Smithers, whose nametag said "MARILYN, Housekeeper."

Grave seemed relieved. "That will be a great help."

"Will there be anything else, sir?" said Smithers.

Grave glanced once more down the line of robots. "I'd like to have a word with the gardener, if you don't mind. The rest can go about their business."

Smithers must have given the robots a secret signal, because they marched away in different directions, each no doubt returning to their duties. The gardener and Smithers remained. Grave glanced at the gardener's nametag.

"Jimmy, is it?" said Grave.

The voice of Jimmy Stewart responded. "Yes, yes it is."

"Tell me, Jimmy, if a rose were to disappear from your garden, would you be aware of it?"

Smithers started to answer for Jimmy, but Grave motioned him to stop. "I'd like to hear from Jimmy."

Jimmy was already uttering a Stewart-like series of "ums" and "wells" and "let me see heres," finally coming to, "Well, yes, yes, I can."

"And have you noticed any roses missing in the last few days? And not bunches of roses, mind, but a single rose?"

Jimmy whirred and shifted back and forth on his feet. "Well, now that you mention it, yes, yes I have, a beautiful one, one of my favorites, in fact, from the bush by the exterior door to the recharging room."

"And I'd be happy to show you that," said Darius Hawthorne, who had come up behind them, startling the three of them, or maybe all four of them. He had no idea where Blunt was.

"Oh," said Grave. "Perfect timing. I was just about to ask about that room."

"Come along, then, I'll give you a tour."

Hawthorne began walking toward what was obviously an open elevator door just off the foyer, no more than twenty steps from where the body was found. Grave, Smithers, and Jimmy, and perhaps Blunt, followed Hawthorne into the elevator. Grave made a mental note to have CSI come back and do a thorough blood and fingerprint analysis of the elevator.

"How is Whitney?" said Grave, trying to make polite elevator conversation, all the while staring at the lighted elevator numbers above the door, which were making a quick trip from "1" to "B."

Hawthorne chuckled. "She's a piece of work, my daughter. When she blows up, she *really* blows up." He held up his right hand, which was crudely bandaged with what looked like a painter's cloth. "Broken frames are sharp."

"You should have that looked at," said Grave. "That bloody rag is doing you no good."

Hawthorne nodded. "More red paint than blood, actually. Anyway, not to worry, about my hand or Whitney. Same thing happened when she went through her mauve squirrel period. We'll make a bonfire of her fish paintings, and then that will be that. Tomorrow, I have no doubt she'll be painting something else and be happy as a clam."

As the door opened, Grave wondered whether she might actually be painting clams by tomorrow and whether she would have the good sense to google clams before she embarked on her clam period. That brief moment of wondering was quickly replaced by a much longer moment of wonder as he took in a room that seemed as impossibly large as it was ultramodern high tech.

Somewhere, Blunt gasped.

21

The room was a symphony of white and stainless steel, accented by a rainbow of snaking wires that provided power to machines with flashing lights of every color and mechanical arms of every function, all aligned in rows and columns throughout the room. The white tile floors gleamed under the fluorescent lights.

"Welcome to my laboratory," said Hawthorne, with a proud sweep of his bandaged hand. "I do testing on prototypes here, as well as minor repairs to the robots. And it's the quickest way to the gardens."

Hawthorne ushered them through the room, pointing out various kinds of equipment, including simple lathes and grinders, as well as more exotic machines of indeterminate function. He paused at a row of a dozen tall glass tubes, and pushed a nearby button. The tubes rotated to reveal an opening tall enough for a man, or a robot. One of the tubes was occupied by what appeared to be a naked man, but was certainly an anatomically correct robot. Its face was turned away from them.

"This is our charging station, where the robots are charged every Friday afternoon. It's a slow trickle charge, so it takes twenty-four hours. And once they're in the tube, they are there for the duration."

Blunt's voice came out of nowhere, as usual. "Is there no override? For example, if a thunderstorm rolled through, and you wanted to prevent damage to them?"

Hawthorne nodded knowingly. "It would have to be quite a

storm—um, who asked that question?"

"Sergeant Blunt," said Grave, waving in the general direction of a cloudlike human.

Hawthorne tried to focus on Blunt, but failed. "Anyway, the answer is yes, but it would have to be quite a storm. We have surge protectors everywhere down here, and it would be quite a bother to interrupt the charging process. We would pretty much have to start all over, which just wouldn't do."

"Noted," said Grave. "And the robot now charging . . ."

"My latest prototype."

Grave glanced up at the prototype. "I had no idea they were so, so. . . "

"Correct in every way?" offered Hawthorne with a broad smile. "My philosophy is, if you're going to do something, do it right, do it thoroughly."

Grave stumbled through his next question. "So they can . . . I mean, in a technical sense, they could . . . um . . ."

Hawthorne slapped him on the back. "Yes, if they were asked, they could do it till their batteries failed."

Grave tried to get his head around that. "Sounds like you could have a whole new business line."

Hawthorne nodded enthusiastically. "Yes, we're in the planning stages. Difficult programming challenge, but we'll see. The importance of foreplay, and so on. Anyway, come along, let's see about that missing rose."

They walked on, Hawthorne picking up the pace, perhaps hoping to avoid more questions, but Grave stopped him in his tracks with one.

"What's that?" Grave pointed at what looked like a microwave oven on steroids.

"Ah," said Hawthorne. "A 3-D printer. Comes in handy when I need a part for one of my prototypes. Cuts development time by months, if not years. Don't know how I ever lived without one."

They continued through the room until they came to an ordinary 6-paned door that obviously led into one of the many gardens that surrounded the mansion. Jimmy shuffled ahead, opened the door, and led them into the garden, which may have had every variety of rose known to man, some budding, some in bloom, some shedding petals.

"Here," said Jimmy, carefully lifting a thorny branch that had obviously been snapped off rather than cut. Whoever did this must have been in a hurry, and taking little heed of the thorns. Grave made a mental note to check everyone's hands for scratches.

He then pulled an evidence tag out of his pocket and looped it around the branch, so the CSI folks would be able to find it when he invited them back to examine the elevator, the lab, and the roses.

"Thank you, Jimmy," he said. "Tell me, what do you think about someone who would take one of your roses?"

Jimmy tilted his head back and forth as if he were weighing his response. "Firstly, he would be a thief, which is bad. Secondly, he lacked training or ignored his training. You don't just snap off a branch like that, which is also bad. Thirdly, he took a rose from my favorite plant, which is neither good nor bad, but clearly means I now have fewer blossoms."

"And how do you *feel* about all that, Jimmy?" Grave held up a hand toward Hawthorne to prevent him from answering for Jimmy, which is exactly what he wanted to do.

"I do not *feel*. I observe, assess, and report, and make whatever corrective actions, if any, that are requested by Mr. Hawthorne or that have been preprogrammed as part of my gardening protocols and defaults."

"Only by Mr. Hawthorne?"

"No, any human."

"And how would you know they were human?"

"Firstly, they have the designated shape, movements, and voice patterns of what is classified as humans."

"Wait," said Grave, glancing over at Hawthorne. "I thought robots made no distinction between man and robot."

Jimmy whirred in a way that only Jimmy Stewart would have whirred in a time of befuddlement, then issued a click, indicating that befuddlement had passed. "True, sir, but humans differ in one significant way—they issue orders, which only humans can do."

Hawthorne seemed relieved, but Grave wasn't through yet. "And if someone issued an order to tear off a branch to your rose bushes, would you do it?"

Jimmy didn't hesitate. "Yes, sir, although I would first advise them that proper technique would require pruning shears."

"But you would do it the wrong way if you were ordered to do so?"

"Yes, of course," said Jimmy. "But why would they do that if I have built-in shears?" He held up his right hand, which immediately transformed into pruning shears.

Grave was surprised, and impressed, but pushed on. "Let's just say that they wanted you to snap off the branch, and not use that wonderful tool of yours. Would you do it?"

Jimmy nodded. "But it would be easier, faster—"

"But you would do it?"

"Yes."

Hawthorne stepped between them. "If there's nothing else, detective, I really should be pressing on to other things."

"Just one last question, if you don't mind."

Hawthorne relented and stepped aside.

"Now, Jimmy, what if you were ordered to *kill* a person?"

Hawthorne jumped in. "We've been over this already, detective. I really *think*—"

"I'd like an answer from Jimmy," said Grave.

Jimmy whirred again, obviously running through his databank of protocols. "*Kill* does not relate to that shape."

Grave was startled. "You mean you *can* kill?"

"Yes, I would follow the ITM Protocol on select garden pests: voles, moles, squirrels, and a variety of crawling, burrowing, and flying insects."

"ITM Protocol?

Hawthorne translated. "It means Intervene to Motionless."

"Yes," added Jimmy, "the ITM Protocol for gardeners."

Grave looked directly at Hawthorne. "For gardeners?"

"Yes, detective," said Hawthorne. "Jimmy has a unique ITM Protocol, as do the other robots."

"And what *shapes* are included for them?"

"I can get you the lists for each robot, but it's probably not pertinent to your investigation. There are only minor differences, but

ITM pests would include primarily pests you'd find in a house and not want: roaches, ants, spiders, and the like."

Grave nodded and turned back to Jimmy. "And tell me, Jimmy, does this protocol require an order from a human to go into effect?"

Jimmy shook his head. "No, it is a default setting, by necessity. To kill a pest, you must act quickly. Otherwise, the opportunity may be lost."

"I see," said Grave. "And how do you kill these *pests*?"

Jimmy spoke in a flat, impersonal tone, as if reading from an instruction manual. "By any means necessary."

22

The tour had ended back in the foyer, Hawthorne and Jimmy walking off in one direction, and Grave, Smithers, and perhaps Blunt walking back to the drawing room, where they found Mrs. Hawthorne seated opposite Grave's chair, knitting away at what looked like a tartan scarf for a giraffe.

Grave had hoped to have a private conversation with Blunt about what they had learned on the tour, but clearly that was not possible. Now that would have to be delayed until the car ride home.

"Blunt, we should be able to wrap up in half an hour or so. I just have to talk with Mrs. Hawthorne here and the young Roy Lynn."

"You'll need permission for Roy Lynn, sir," said Blunt, already knowing what would be required of him. "I'll track down Ms. Waters, then."

Grave could tell by the flapping sound of Blunt's shoes that he was leaving the room, the sound fading quickly to near nothingness as Blunt ascended the stairs to Whitney's studio.

Grave motioned Smithers to his tape recorder position and then assumed his own position seated opposite Mrs. Hawthorne, who continued to clack away with her knitting needles.

Philomena Hawthorne, second wife of Darius Hawthorne and sister to Chester Clink, the notorious serial killer, was a handsome woman, but certainly no trophy wife. Fortyish, tall and slender, with mouse brown hair done up in a tight bun, and clothed all in black, from her tight, knee-length skirt to her wrinkle-covering turtleneck, to her black, sensible walking shoes, to her black leggings, she appeared to be more of a goth spinster than the wife of a high-tech baron. Her face was thin and angular, with a prominent, slightly hooked nose between darkly golden eyes that looked out on the world with a blankness that Grave had never seen before, her eyebrows seemingly locked into a position that suggested no one was at home. She appeared to have no lips at all, so tight and controlled were her expressions. In short, if people were paintings, she was a blank canvas, or nearly so.

The few brush strokes that were Philomena Hawthorne now set aside the knitting project and stared up at Grave, her long fingers laced together in front of her face.

"Detective," she said. "I trust we can do this quickly."

Grave was about to reply in the affirmative—he really did want to get this phase of the investigation over with, so he could enjoy what remained of the weekend, which wasn't much—but he was distracted by the sound of rapidly approaching footsteps. The sound reminded him of a sequence on *Sesame Street*, when Grover, one of the many Muppets that had helped define his childhood, was attempting to explain the difference between "near" and "far" by running from a position far away from the camera to a position close up, when his face filled the screen and he would shout out, "Near!" The only difference was the sound was more like the sound made by the rapidly flapping feet of Sergeant Blunt, who now burst into the room, startling everyone in the room except Mrs. Hawthorne, who seemed to expect the intrusion, or at least was not easily surprised by a door bursting open with the concomitant, near-disembodied voice of Sergeant Blunt.

"Sir," said Blunt, gasping for breath. "It's Ms. Waters. She's dead."

23

"It's almost like performance art," said Polk, pointing at the lifeless body of Whitney Waters.

"What do you mean?" said Grave.

"Don't you see it? She's been positioned on the canvas of a painting in progress. See here, just to the left of her hip, the roughed in outline of a massive herring."

"Mackerel," said Grave.

"Whatever. One of her fish, you see. Her signature fish."

"How do you know about her fish?"

Polk beamed. "Well, it may surprise you, but I am a bit of a collector. I have three of her paintings. And now they're worth at least twice what I paid for them."

"How lucky for you."

The sarcasm flew over Polk's head and rocketed away. "And now you have not just a painting, you have the artist and the painting together, as one. Performance art. This canvas is going to be worth a bundle."

Grave didn't really know where Polk was headed with this—a dead artist would have a relatively limited ability to perform—but he had to admit that the body had been positioned intentionally, arms and legs splayed as with the first body, but without the arrow or the happy face. Indeed, the body had been drenched with what must have been an entire bucket of red paint, which had covered the body and splashed and pooled around it along with the slightly darker blood. And, of course, there was her severed hand, which had been drenched in paint and pressed down in several places to create handprints on the canvas. If anyone was doing the performing, it was the killer.

"And just look at this chaos," said Polk. The room had indeed changed dramatically. Paintings and broken paintings were scattered helter-skelter around the room. Whitney's easel was lying on its side. Her palette was stuck to one of the windows, clearly thrown with some force. There had been some modest attempts at cleaning—a few of the busted paintings had been repositioned on the walls—but the theme of the day was chaos.

"A lot of this is from a temper tantrum thrown by Whitney, er, Ms. Waters," said Grave.

"Really? And why was that?" said Polk.

"Not important. Let's just say she couldn't handle the truth, at least not well."

"Humph."

"So," said Grave, "what do you think?"

Polk shrugged, but not in a casual way, as if to express dismay or indifference, but in a wholly professional way, as if to suggest that he had a definite answer but he wasn't about to give the totality of his thoughts away to just anyone, particularly Detective Simon Grave. "I think we'll find similarities and differences."

Grave threw up his hands. "Well, thank you for the clarity."

Polk chuckled. "Sorry, but you do ask for it at times."

"Please, I need your thoughts."

Polk began pointing. "See here, the faint bruise on the right cheek. She's been slugged, probably to the point of unconsciousness. Certainly a broken jaw. Then, I think he took his time arranging this tableau."

"And cause of death?"

"More paint than blood, so I think we'll find a small puncture wound on her back when we turn her over, with most of the bleeding internal, as with the Jones woman. I'll give you a call when I know for sure."

"Speaking of calls," said Grave, "you never called about the missing hand. Anything on the security cameras?"

"Oh, yes," said Polk. "I was about to call you when the call came in about the second body. I can show you the tape when you come down to the morgue tomorrow, but we definitely caught the image of someone coming and going. The image is dark and not very clear, but perhaps it will mean more to you than it does to me. The puzzling thing is how he—or she—managed to get through three locked doors to get to the hand."

"Inside job, perhaps?"

"Don't be ridiculous," said Polk. "Only four people have keys, and none of them could possibly be involved in this."

"All right, then, another piece of the puzzle."

24

News of Whitney's death had spread quickly throughout the mansion, as well as through the carnival outside, with predictable results. Hawthorne walked away in silence when he heard the news, unable to speak. Roy Lynn was devastated, in shock, and had been quickly taken away by Ms. LaFarge, who had also been shocked by the news. Philomena, on the other hand, had shown no obvious emotions, but had managed to twist her face into a deep frown. Edwina, of course, just sat there, expressionless as usual. Grave had thought to pull her aside and invoke his restorative accent, but had thought better of it. This family, if you could call it that, was in shock and mourning, and needed some space, so after giving instructions to Smithers that he would return the next day to continue his interviews, he and Blunt left, leaving Polk and the uniforms to finish up.

They raced to the car. Fortunately, the media crews were talking excitedly among themselves, as if the news of Whitney's death was a gift from heaven, and didn't notice them leaving until it was too late, the car spraying gravel on all who attempted to pursue them.

On a normal workday, they would have headed back to the precinct to discuss the case and brief Captain Morgan on their progress. But it was Sunday, so they would have to discuss the case as Blunt drove Grave home.

"Something's fishy," said Blunt, breaking a silence that had lasted half the way to Grave's house, both of them deep in thought.

"Fishy? How do you mean?"

"It just doesn't add up. I mean, the whole happy face thing with Ms. Jones's body was clearly an attempt by the killer to implicate Ms. Waters."

Grave was not sure where Blunt was headed. "So?"

"If you dislike Ms. Waters so much in the first place, why bother trying to set her up, when you could just kill her outright?"

"I see your point, but maybe killing her wasn't enough. Maybe he wanted to make her suffer first, with the killing of her lover."

"Possibly, but . . ."

"But you think we may be dealing with two killers."

"Yes, sir, a copycat of sorts."

"But why?"

They both pondered this quietly for some seconds, Grave the first to break silence.

"Or perhaps Whitney's death wasn't planned at all."

"And something went wrong with the plan?"

"Yes, exactly."

They grew silent once more, Blunt making the final turn to Grave's house.

"What about the robots, then?" said Blunt.

Grave wasn't sure how to answer. Hawthorne's assurances seemed to eliminate them. On the other hand, this whole ITM protocol business was disturbing. These robots *could* kill, at least if the shape of the victim was right. And Grave didn't trust machines of any kind to begin with. He was certain, in fact, that his toaster was a sentient being, albeit a sadistic, toast-burning one.

"Part of me says yes, part of me says no."

"I agree, sir. I mean, they're so *human*. The way they look, the way they move. Most people would never guess they weren't real. So who's to say they couldn't kill?"

The car rolled up in front of Grave's house, an old two-bedroom bungalow he'd bought from a house flipper six months ago. On the outside it looked like a freshly painted old house with a few new trees planted here and there. On the inside, it was a miracle of stainless steel, granite, and gleaming hardwoods, with all the niceties required to jack up the price and assure a tidy profit. Grave had snapped it up the first day it was on the market.

"Here you go, sir."

Grave got out, closed the door, and then leaned in to the open window. "I'm going to drive myself to the morgue tomorrow morning. You're welcome to come along."

"In your car, sir?" There was more than a note of disgust and a symphony of horror in his voice.

Grave glanced over at the little red car parked in his driveway. Blunt had been in the car only once, but apparently speed thrill in a sardine can was not his idea of fun. Grave let him off the hook. "We could meet there if you like."

"If it's all the same to you, sir, I'd rather meet you at the precinct. Blowing the whole weekend means I have a lot of errands to run first thing."

"Very well." Grave turned and walked toward the house. Dark clouds were rolling in and a wind had come up. *Oh, great,* he thought. *A storm. Just what I need.*

The rain began to fall, hard.

He looked at his car again. Its canvas top was not just down, but off, packed away behind the seats, one of the ingenious ways the Austin Healey folks had used to assure that all its drivers got the aerobic exercise they needed each day, particularly on rainy days.

He ran for the car.

25

Grave couldn't tell whether the loud buzzing noise was coming from his head, his car's forty-hamster engine, or its ever-on radio, featuring the stylistic ramblings of Reverend Bendigo Bottoms, who despite the buzz, or perhaps *because* of the buzz, was railing on this morning about the ungodliness of emoji use.

"I was okay with the happy face, that was good, and wholly godly, but now the evil that is the internet has unleashed the Devil's hordes, an emoji for anger, for jealousy, for deceit, for pride. Oh, yes it has, and we shall have none of it!"

Grave didn't know how he felt about emoji. On one level, they were cute. On another level, the sub-basement, he had no idea how to insert any of them on his Facebook page, so he was jealous of his fellow Facebookers. *Was there really an emoji for jealousy?*

He drove on. Having the top down on the car was beginning to help, the breeze dampening the buzzing in his head as it whisked away, as best it could, the near overwhelming smell of the mildew that had blossomed in the carpeting from last night's rain.

Grave had spent the previous evening mulling over the case with the help of his new favorite wine, Duct Tape Chardonnay, "the wine that can fix anything," an inexpensive wine that had never touched oak, or perhaps even grapes. His mulling had yielded nothing new, but he was now fully versed in the promotional copy on the wine's label, including its place of fermentation and bottling: Hoboken, New Jersey. The pain in his head suggested that he should have stopped at two glasses. The blaring horns suggested he was driving too slowly, and perhaps shouldn't be behind the wheel at all, but he persisted, finally pulling into one of the many available parking spaces at the morgue, which apparently was no one's destination of choice.

The familiar smell of the examination room and the sudden glimpse of Whitney's tabled body as he entered made him want to turn on his heels, go outside, and retch. But Polk's calm voice pulled him in.

"Just as we thought, Grave," he said, motioning Grave closer. "See here, the same entry wound."

Grave looked down at Whitney's body, beautiful even in death. He felt a sense of guilt and remorse that the last words he'd said to her had led her up the stairs to the room where she would die among paintings depicting the wrong fish. He looked down at the wound, and nodded. "It's the same."

"*Same* doesn't quite cover it. It's *identical*, or nearly so. Angle and depth are the same. Location's a bit off, but no more than a few millimeters."

Grave was one of those detectives who didn't believe in coincidence, but unlike most of his colleagues, he reserved the right to accept it as a real possibility, thinking if it wasn't possible, why was there a word for it?

Polk rambled on. "It's astounding, really. To get the exact depth, you'd have to remember the first victim's wound and make allowances for differences in muscle tone and density. No, *more*, you'd have to *feel* the differences even as you were thrusting the icepick in."

"But wouldn't the handle of the icepick dictate the depth?"

"To some extent, yes, but every icepick handle I've ever seen is rounded at the grip, meaning the depth could vary as much as half an inch, depending on the power behind the thrust."

"Well, what then?"

"It's as if the killer *sensed* the depth," said Polk. "Like a machine—or a *robot*—programmed to do just that."

Grave and Polk gave each other the kind of look that is usually accompanied by a hundred violins trying to simulate raised eyebrows.

Polk was having none of it, however. "Wait, robots can't kill.

Smirnoff's Law and all of that."

Grave didn't want to get into another discussion about what robots could or couldn't do. "It's Asimov's Law, actually, but I really don't have time to discuss it. I'm expected at the station."

Polk didn't like being challenged, even when he was clearly wrong, but he took the mistake in stride. "Whatever, but before you go, there's two things. First, a man claiming to be the brother of Epiphany Jones came to identify and claim her body this morning. Just before you arrived, in fact. I can't believe you didn't see him on your way in."

Grave didn't remember seeing anyone, in the building or the parking lot. "No, sorry, and how could he possibly know she was here?"

Polk had already considered this. "I suspect that someone at the mansion gave him a call. Seems like a natural thing to do, notifying the relatives."

Grave nodded and then had another thought. "You didn't release the body to him, did you?" He glanced furtively around the room. All the other examination tables were empty.

Polk was clearly annoyed that Grave would even think that. "Of course not. I need orders for that."

"Well, where is she, then?"

"Drawer Six," he said, pointing to the bank of drawers on the far wall.

"Good, good," said Grave. "So, how did this supposed brother react when you turned him down?"

"He just asked about the possible timing of the release—I told him a few days, perhaps a week or so—and he said he'd stay in town until he could claim her body."

"And did he say where he would be staying?"

"No."

Grave considered the possibilities, which ranged from outrageously expensive to dirt cheap. "The Hilton over on Ames, perhaps?"

Polk shook his head. "No, no, no. Think cheaper."

Grave went to the other end of the spectrum. "Surely not the Inn and Out?"

Polk nodded. "I would think so, although really, even they may have turned him away. He was not exactly a snappy dresser. More like a guy who would live in a van down by the river." He laughed self-appreciatively at the connection he had made with that old, tired *Saturday Night Live* routine.

Grave gave him a halfhearted smile. "Are we done here, then?"

"Not by a long shot," said Polk. "Have you forgotten the security cam footage?"

He had, in fact. "Oh, right. Let's do that."

Polk led him out of the examination room and down a long, gray corridor to a door marked "Security. Authorized Personnel Only." The little room was crammed with electronic gadgets, including six monitors providing live-stream coverage of hallways few people would ever want to walk down.

Sitting behind a console filled with buttons, toggles, and flashing lights was a heavy-set man in a security guard uniform, stuffing his mouth with what looked like a breakfast sandwich of some kind. The room smelled of bacon and overcooked eggs, and given the number of wrappers lying on the console, the sandwich was one of several that had given up the ghost this morning. The man glanced at them, stood, and left the room without a word, chewing as he went and closing the door behind him, his departure covered in excruciating detail on one of the monitors as he waddled slowly down the hall. There was a brief burst of sunlight as he pushed open an exterior door and stepped outside.

Polk sat down, brushed the wrappers aside, pushed a few buttons, toggled a few toggles, and sat back with a satisfied grunt as a video appeared on the central monitor. "Here you go."

They watched as a dark figure moved slowly down the hallway to the examination room. As he pushed through the door, he glanced back to make sure he wasn't being followed, his face briefly appearing full on before he disappeared into the room.

"Roll it back a bit," said Grave.

Polk fiddled with a switch or two, and the video began to run backwards.

"Stop there," said Grave, Polk quickly complying, freezing the frame on the man's face.

"Wait, that's not possible," said Polk.

"Oh, but it is," said Grave.

"But that's—"

"Peter O'Toole," said Grave.

The only question was . . . which one?

26

As much as he wanted to race to the station and share his startling news with Blunt and Captain Morgan, the equally unexpected appearance of Epiphany's brother had taken him to the Inn and Out, a motel not just located on the other side of the tracks, but on the other side of the other side of the tracks.

The motel did not appear to be doing much business. Only two cars were parked in front of the long line of doors leading to the shabby rooms that typically rented by the hour. Apparently, even the hookers had moved on, and the condition of the cars suggested that one, perhaps both, had been abandoned there years ago. A neon sign in the office window flashed "VA_CY," the "CAN" burnt out of the sign, perhaps the whole motel.

The clerk, a thin bald man who had apparently left the realm of CAN many years ago appeared reluctantly from a back room after Grave had endlessly rung the desk bell, Grave's hand moving so rapidly that the little bell didn't even have time to ring, but instead responded with a metal-on-metal clack.

The man pulled the bell away from Grave. "Whatcha want?"

Grave's fingers still tingled a bit from the bell-clacking exercise. "I'm looking for a man," he began.

"You'd want the Winkin', Blinkin' and Nod down the street."

"No," said Grave, a bit nonplussed by the misunderstanding. "I'm a detective, looking for a man." He pulled out his badge and showed it to the clerk, who took a step back.

"Whoa, now, Mr. Detective, there's nothin' goin' on here. We're just a law-abidin' rest stop for weary travelers."

Grave wondered how many times the man had used that line. "Of course you are. Look, the man has done nothing wrong. You and your, um, *motel* have done nothing wrong. I just want to talk to him about a case I'm working."

The man relaxed, at least somewhat. He remained a step back from the counter. "Nobody here. We're full empty."

That is not the news Grave wanted to here. "No one?"

"Nope."

"Has anyone inquired about a room, then?"

The clerk nodded. "That guy," he said, pointing to one of the cars in the parking lot. "I guess $32.50 a night is too expensive for him."

Grave thanked the clerk and walked out into the parking lot. The first car, an old white Corvair, was empty, as was the second car, a shark-finned Plymouth, a battleship of a car from the age of Sputnik. Two cars, no man. Who had the clerk been pointing at?

He looked around in all directions, finally spotting a man at the far end of the parking lot, walking toward a whitewashed cinderblock building, a little restaurant called the Skunk 'n Donuts, one of several around town. A large neon sign on the roof simulated a blue skunk squirting a green liquid cloud into the air, which then magically transformed into a red neon donut that flashed three times before the sequence repeated.

Appetizing, thought Grave. He trotted across the parking lot, jumped the curb, and climbed a few feet up a dirt embankment to reach the restaurant. The man already had a cup of coffee in his hand and was making his way from the counter to a booth at the back. Other than Grave, he was the only customer.

"Help you, mister?" said the teenager behind the counter. A skunk-shaped nametag indicated that his name was JERRY. His jaunty white paper hat, complete with skunk logo, gave the impression that he was a young soldier about to board a train to the front, a brave member of the Skunk Battalion.

Grave scanned the donut racks, looking for his go-to donut, chocolate glazed, but saw only two choices, plain and powdered, and even those in limited quantities, *limited* being three each.

"Baker's sick today," said Jerry. "These are yesterday's, but they're half price."

"That's okay," said Grave. "Just coffee."

Jerry seemed relieved. "Great. Just be a second." He pulled a Styrofoam cup from a dispenser and moved down the counter to a row of coffee pots, all half-filled with what looked like diesel fuel.

Grave paid for the coffee and walked to the booth at the back. "By any chance are you Mr. Jones?" he said, hovering over the man and flashing his badge.

The man seemed startled at first, but then relaxed. "Yes, that's me. What, is this about my sister?"

Grave could see the family resemblance, particularly the blue eyes, which seemed vacant. He wondered briefly whether Epiphany's hair was naturally blond—there was certainly no clue from her body, which was free of pubic hair or stubble of any kind, shaved clean for a special meeting, perhaps. Her brother's hair, by contrast, was near jet black and combed back into the ducktails of a bygone era. His nose had clearly been broken several times, its angle changing direction as dramatically and frequently as a slalom run. It was hard to tell how tall he was, but basketball was certainly a sport he never played.

He was clearly on the down and out, his white t-shirt tending toward gray, his beard of a scraggily ilk, his face greasy and unwashed. In short, if people were logos, he would have been the logo for the Inn and Out.

Grave nodded. "I'm Detective Simon Grave. And, I'm sorry, I don't really have your full name?"

"Oh, I thought you knew. I'm Calamity Jones, Piph's brother. Just call me Cal."

Grave never ceased to be amazed at the cruelty parents imposed on their children just by the simple act of naming them. *Epiphany? Calamity?* Gads! Even Cal "Rhymes with Dow" Jones was a disaster. Yes, Grave had had to deal with all the Simon Says jokes, but still, *Calamity?*

"May I join you?"

Jones nodded and motioned for him to sit down. "Of course."

Grave slipped into the booth opposite Cal, started to take a sip of coffee, thought better of it, and set it aside. "First, please accept my sincerest condolences for your loss. She was by all accounts a wonderful young woman, and—"

Cal laughed out loud, head to ceiling. "Who have you been *talking* to? She was a bitch on wheels. Beautiful in her way, but a true bitch of the first order."

"Sorry," said Grave, "just trying to—"

"Be polite? No worries here. She was what she was," he said, adding, "and now she's not." There seemed to be not a trace of sadness or loss.

Grave asked a question he knew the answer to already. "Were you close?"

"Not for many, many years."

"And when was the last time the two of you spoke?"

Cal slumped back in the booth. "Let me see, let me see—oh—it must have been a month ago, I guess. I was having a run of bad luck, and needed a spot of cash."

Given the look of him, Grave couldn't imagine that went well. "How did that go?"

"Look at me, detective." He shook his head. "Not well at all."

"Did you speak of anything else?"

Cal smiled slyly. "Of course. You know how it goes, if you want something from someone, you don't just jump to that. You ease into the conversation. Ask them how they are and so forth."

"And how was she?"

Cal paused a few seconds. "You know, I really don't know. She said all the right things. I'm fine and so on. But there was something about her voice, almost a sadness, perhaps a trace of ennui, with a dash of world-weariness, and—"

"I see," said Grave, pulling out his notebook. "Do you mind if I ask you a few more questions about your sister?"

Cal shrugged. "Not at all." He began to drum his fingers on the table as if he were late to an appointment.

27

Clues come at you willy-nilly, when you least expect them. Cal's dark hair had been an epiphany about Epiphany. She had been clean shaven at the time of her death. Not a hint of stubble under her arms, on her legs, or even on her groin, as was the fashion of the day. *Perhaps she was lured to the mansion that night,* Grave thought. *Or perhaps that was her normal routine for a Friday night.*

He slowed the car, downshifting to second, and made the left at Monroe Avenue, which would take him to the precinct. He had missed Bendigo Bottom's latest Eleventh Commandment, but the gospel music gave him all the energy he needed to lift himself up, albeit at full volume, pedestrians stopping in their tracks to watch him drive by, seemingly on a mobile mission from god.

There had not been much to learn from his interview with Cal Jones. He was the only living relative. He knew very little about Piph's daily routine, her business, or even her friends. He wasn't the least surprised about her affair with Whitney—she had been a declared bisexual since high school. But the only relationship Piph had talked about was a relationship she was having with a man—who, she wouldn't say. Something about a potentially lucrative art deal. Uncharacteristically, she had promised Cal some cash if the deal went through. Cal thought it must have been one hell of a deal, because Piph was not known for her generosity. Grave had given Cal his card and asked him to call if he remembered anything that might help with the case, and in any event, to call him once he'd found a place to stay, which may have been in his car, down by the river.

Grave pulled into a vacant parking spot at the precinct's front entrance, and climbed out of the car, his legs stiff from his run across the Inn and Out parking lot. He really needed to start an exercise program.

As he climbed the steps, thighs screaming, his cellphone rang. It was his father, who seemed unusually animated and exorcised about something.

"Simon, is that you?"

"Yes, of course it's me."

"Good, I think I've got something that may be of help, maybe solve the whole damn thing."

"What?"

"About the Clinks. It's a bit complicated. Could you come over tonight?"

"Um, Dad, if it's so important, why not just tell me now?"

"No, it's something you have to see. Photos for you to look at."

He had learned long ago not to argue with his father. "All right, be mysterious. I'll see you about six or so." He rang off, continuing up the steps and pushing through the door.

Every time he came into the front entrance of the Crab Cove Station House, which was rare, he had the feeling that he had jumped into a painting by Bruegel, scores of people scurrying about, doing so many things you couldn't quite focus on any single one. You had to stand there and take it all in. There was the usual lineup of pained relatives sitting on a bench waiting to talk to an officer about what their son or daughter had done, despite their best parenting advice. There were uniformed officers at desks, taking statements, their fingers poised over keyboards, getting ready to take down the next statement with the hunt-and-peck skills of a child learning Chopsticks on the piano. There was the coffee pot in the corner, always empty, and a large empty box that had once contained donuts, his favorite long gone, snapped up by an eager competitor who had claimed dibs on it the moment he had arrived at the station. There was the air itself, as if the station had its own atmosphere, one composed of angst, sweat, and just enough oxygen to keep most people awake. And then there was the "fishbowl," the glassed-in office of Captain Henry

Morgan, known affectionately, when affection was called for, as "Cap'n Hank."

This morning, Cap'n Hank was standing behind his desk, motioning for Grave to join him and what might have been Sergeant Blunt in his office. He looked upset. No Cap'n Hank this morning. Captain Henry Morgan loomed in his place, looking all the part of a privateer sizing up a merchant ship to be taken as bounty.

The first fusillade always came as the door to Morgan's office was opened. He wanted everyone to know who he was upset with, but not why.

"Get in here, goddammit!"

Grave stepped in and closed the door. He knew without looking back that every officer outside the fishbowl was leaning toward it, trying to hear what might happen next. "Good morning, Captain."

"Is it, now?" said Morgan, motioning Grave into one of two office chairs, the other already taken up by Sergeant Blunt, who was no more than a sheepish, contrite cloud and dutifully silent.

Morgan plopped down into his chair, rocking it back and forth menacingly, as if he were about to launch himself across the desk at Grave. He was a man as wide as he was tall, which was considerable, with a neck as wide as his head, giving him a look, complete with crewcut, that most people would characterize as the look of a blockhead, not that anyone who valued their life would ever say that to him. He had dark eyes, like a shark, and a nose that suggested blunt force trauma, the large blob of flesh near flattened to his face. If you looked closely, which was never recommended, you would have seen a slightly cleft lip and the attendant shiny scars of a poorly done operation. Morgan had grown a moustache to help cover it up, but that had only emphasized it, the scar appearing like the beginnings of a crop circle slashed through the close-cropped brush of gray hair.

All of this—this man, this force, this menace—was stuffed into a uniform wrinkled permanently at every flex point, despite the best efforts of the dry cleaners. In short, if he had been wearing a plumed tricorn hat, you would have sworn you were looking at the eponymous seventeenth-century privateer himself, with or without the visionary help of rum.

Grave tried not to look into the captain's eyes, where nothing good awaited, but instead focused on the display shelves behind the man and the various Captain Morgan Rum souvenirs and collectibles given to him by various officers and dignitaries for his many birthdays.

Morgan caught him not looking. "Look at me, dammit!"

Grave complied, waiting for the assault, which was already proceeding.

"Guess who called me this morning?" snarled Morgan.

"The mayor?"

Captain Morgan slapped his hand on the desk, which seemed to bounce off the floor. "The *mayor* was only the beginning. I've also heard from the heads of the Chamber of Commerce, the Rotary Club, the Yacht Club, the Elks, the Legion, the Lions, and the fuckin' *chess club* at the high school!"

"Well, sir—"

"Quiet! I've also heard from none other than Darius Hawthorne himself, our little town's captain of industry, the man who provides jobs to hundreds of people, without which we wouldn't be a fuckin' town."

Grave tried to speak again, to point out that tourists were the town's main source of revenue, but Morgan held up a hand.

"And do you know what they all want to know, detective?"

Grave didn't dare jump in.

"They want to know what *imbecile* would think people in a locked room would be prime suspects in a murder that occurred *outside* that room while they were locked *inside* that room."

"Sir, if I may, you've forgotten—"

"The second murder? No, I have not forgotten it, because your failure to pursue outside suspects is at least partly responsible, maybe *completely* responsible. While you interviewed the innocent, the killer was on the loose, carrying out his dastardly plan." Morgan slumped back into his chair, his eyebrows raised to full staff, challenging Grave to counter the undeniable logic and ineluctable truth of what he had just said.

Grave gathered himself, pushing down the question of when he had last heard the word *dastardly* used in a sentence, and returned to the question at hand, namely what Morgan had indeed forgotten.

"Sir, what you have forgotten is not the second murder, as *dastardly* as it was, but an important element of the *first* murder, namely the simultaneous disappearance of the MacGuffin Trophy from that same locked room."

"What are you saying?" said Captain Morgan.

"Sir, if a trophy can disappear from a locked room, why not a person? And if a person can disappear from a room, he can also get back into that room after committing a theft and a murder, creating what apparently many in this community think is a foolproof alibi."

Morgan began to speak, then stopped, logic tripping over facts in his mind, leaving him more puzzled. Thankfully, though, his anger seemed to have abated.

"So you think there is some kind of secret doorway in the room?" He seemed incredulous.

"Yes, sir. It's a very old mansion, and certainly large enough to conceal any number of secret passageways."

Words began to emerge from the obscure mouth of the fuzzy mountain of a man sitting next to Grave. "Sorry, sir, but I've gone over every inch of that room—every wall, the floor, the ceiling, and anything that might be pushed or pulled to open such a door, and there's nothing."

Grave's mind, hangover-inhibited as it was, tried its best to grapple with the problem, but the best solution it could come up with was that an invisible man similar in ability to Sergeant Blunt had taken the trophy out of the room, locked everyone in, and then killed Epiphany Jones. Of course, that would mean that no one in the room had happened to notice a trophy floating across the room and out the door.

Captain Morgan sensed Grave's confusion. "Obviously, we're missing something. Something that was said or done but missed, or something that was said or done but misunderstood. Start at the beginning, Grave, and leave nothing out."

28

Say what you will about Captain Morgan, and most people did, he was much more than an irascible blockhead. He had an uncanny ability to process, sort, and concatenate facts to reach logical solutions. The downside of this ability was that he offered solutions after each known fact, not waiting for the totality of the information before reaching conclusions. The effect in many cases was that by the end of a case review, he would have identified as many as twenty suspects who had "definitely" done it, whatever the crime might be. Watching him work was like watching a child on Christmas morning opening present after present, each one better than the next, but each quickly set aside for the next and the next, the very last present, the one hidden behind the tree, declared the absolute best.

The problem with his approach was that it tended to create a solution based on a chain of logic, rather than on a chain of evidence, which could lead to grave misunderstandings of what had actually happened. In that respect, it was much like the game "telephone," where a chain of people transmit a short sentence down the chain. Each person hears the sentence differently, so that by the time the last person in the chain announces what the first person said, the message may have changed from "apples are good for you" to "crap cars would too."

So by the end of their hour-long conversation, which involved a discussion of the crime scene and each person interviewed, as well as speculation about motive, means, and opportunity, Captain Morgan had identified the killer as Whitney Waters—"clearly she put the emoji on the body, so it must be her"—Roy Lynn Waters—"the arrow clinches it"—Darius Hawthorne—"people in turtlenecks have something to hide"—Lola LaFarge—"you can't trust Frenchies"— Edwina Hawthorne—"perhaps no one was looking down and she wheeled herself out of the room, the trophy tucked safely under her wheelchair"—Smithers—"well, of course, it was the butler"— Philomena Hawthorne—"Clink's sister, she must have done it"— Calamity Jones—"a man with a name like that is capable of anything"—Whitney Waters again—"she had motive and opportunity and, um , wait, she's dead."

In the end, they had managed to do a complete mashup of Sir Arthur Conan Doyle's famous line, "Once you eliminate the impossible, whatever remains, no matter how improbable, must be the truth." The result of their deduction by committee had changed it to read, "Once you eliminate the truth, whatever remains, no matter how improbable, must be the impossible."

Although everyone agreed that everyone had done it, that particular solution was not in the least bit helpful. Grave had then brought Blunt and Morgan up to speed on the morgue video and his father's mysterious case closer, the first invoking a shout of "robots!" from Captain Morgan, the second, a silent head-shaking. Morgan had never been a fan of Grave's father.

Ultimately, they decided that Grave would return to the mansion to finish up his interviews, while Blunt proceeded to Ramrod Robotics. The three of them weren't sure whether anyone in the Hawthorne household could be trusted to give them objective information about the robots, so Blunt's job was to verify what they had been told about the robots and also gather what additional information he could about robots before returning to the mansion to help Grave interview each of the robots, as well as their inventor-master, Darius Hawthorne, and his wife, Philomena.

Captain Morgan had been particularly upset that Grave had not checked out Ms. Jones's apartment and gallery on Saturday, so he instructed Grave and Blunt to check out both as soon as the interviews were completed. He'd send CSI over to get things started.

If they completed everything in a timely manner, they were to return to the precinct. Otherwise, Grave would proceed to his father's house to learn what the elder Grave might have discovered or deduced, if anything. Barring a break in the case, the three of them would then meet the next morning to discuss further steps. Meanwhile, Captain Morgan would do what captains do, namely sit in the fishbowl and stare menacingly into the outer office.

Each scurried to their tasks, Morgan's requiring the least scurrying, of course, as per the privileges of his rank. He did manage to pick up the phone and give Ramrod Robotics a call to alert them to the arrival of a man they may or may not be able to see, and then he settled back in a chair that had molded itself to his broad, hemorrhoid-rich bottom, and watched the swirl of activity outside the fishbowl.

29

Grave glanced at his watch, or at least the wrist where the watch was known to reside, and saw only a band of pale flesh where the watch should have been. He must have left it on the nightstand when he stumbled out of the house this morning. So now, mostly clueless about the time and clearly watch-free, he climbed into his little Sprite to head back to the mansion. The car started up with a sucking sound, like a drowning man gasping for air, before the gospel music overwhelmed it. Part of him wanted it to be the sound of a death rattle, so he could move on to something resembling modern transportation, but he knew that until the wheels fell off, he would have to live with the little red gift from his father, who treasured the car even now and asked about it in the way that a grandfather might ask about his favorite grandson, not that he had any, the Sprite itself discouraging any relationship that might produce one.

The case was driving him mad. How are the robots involved? Who is controlling the robots? Where is the MacGuffin Trophy? How could it have possibly disappeared from a locked room? What's the deal with the missing hand? Why would anyone name a donut place Skunk 'n Donuts? And for that matter, who's the miscreant who gloms onto the chocolate donut every morning?

These and other questions occupied his mind as he drove his gospel choir to the mansion, his mind so focused that when he arrived at the steps of the mansion, he had no memory of the drive at all, save for the voice of Bendigo Bottoms, which had broken the spell of his reverie.

"Life is like a tuna fish sandwich—"

Grave turned off the ignition, the voice of Bendigo Bottoms stopping abruptly, which Grave instantly regretted. Now he had yet another question on his mind: why *is* life like a tuna fish sandwich? His stomach had a related question: *where* is my tuna fish sandwich?

Distracted, he didn't see the headlong rush of Claire Fairly, who was upon him as soon as he climbed out of the car.

"Detective, a word please," she said, whipping her microphone around, the cameraman positioning himself to get the two of them in the frame, with the mansion as background.

Claire Fairly had been the bane of his existence on cases beyond number, shadowing him mercilessly from crime scene to crime scene, her slanted, fact-obscured reports helping her move up the communications ladder from reporter to sometime anchor. Now she apparently had her sights on evening anchor, the plum of local news, the next step on her quest for a national media job.

Whether that was possible was unclear. The beautiful reporter he had met years ago was now fading, crow's feet and frown lines etched into her face, her once-lustrous blond hair having given way to the consistency of straw, her eyes tired-looking and rheumy. She was still tall and shapely in her way, but the effects of gravity had taken their toll. The deep-dive dresses of her youth, which had emphasized her breasts and improved her ratings, had been replaced by high-necked dresses and scarves to hide the ravages of time. In short, if reporters were clowns, Claire Fairly would have been praised for her distinctive makeup and the uncanny way she had been able to transform herself into the woman she once was, at least on camera.

Grave tried to push by her without comment, but she persisted. "Do you have any suspects? A description? Anything?"

He pulled out one of his go-to responses, a response he knew would rankle her. "All will be revealed in the course of time."

"And *when* will that be?" There was more than a note of frustration in her voice, tinged perhaps with a lightly veiled implication that he was not doing his job.

"I think I just answered that, Ms. Fairly." He pushed past her and walked slowly up the steps, not wanting to give her the satisfaction of seeing him fleeing her questioning, which he was.

His stomach rumbled, no doubt seeking the answer to its question about the availability of a tuna fish sandwich, a question quickly answered as Grave stepped into the foyer, where Smithers stood holding a silver tray laden with two cups of coffee and a carefully stacked pyramid of crust-free sandwiches. Grave caught a glimpse of Marilyn, the housekeeping syndroid, walking up the staircase as seductively as anyone who looks like Peter O'Toole could manage.

"Good day, sir," said Smithers, bowing his head slightly. "The drawing room awaits, as does Mrs. Hawthorne."

Grave noticed Polk at the far end of the foyer with the CSI team, which had been called back in to gather additional evidence in the foyer, the elevator, Hawthorne's lab, and the garden. He nodded at Polk, who dutifully nodded back and then turned away to get back to his task.

Grave followed Smithers into the drawing room, where Mrs. Hawthorne was hard at work on her giraffe scarf, which was now at least a foot longer. Perhaps a T-Rex was the intended recipient. She was wearing the exact same clothes she had worn the day before. Curious, particularly for a woman of wealth, but these were stressful times, and each person dealt with grief in different ways.

Philomena set aside her knitting and took a cup of coffee and a little multilayered sandwich involving various soft cheeses off the tray. Smithers then turned the tray toward Grave. There wasn't a single tuna fish sandwich, so he selected one with deviled ham and popped it into his mouth, where it lingered only briefly. His coffee was prepared just as he liked it, namely as a beverage that was actually coffee and not whatever that liquid was that came out of the pot back at the precinct.

He took a sip, nodded his thanks to Smithers, and sat down.

"Madam," he began. "Might we continue?"

Philomena set her coffee and sandwich aside. "Detective," she said, repeating the words she had said in the first interview, "I trust we can do this quickly."

Her voice and appearance showed no signs of grief, but Grave followed grief protocol, anyway. "First, let me say how sorry I am about the loss of your daughter. She was—"

"*Step*daughter," she said curtly, correcting him. "And let me make myself clear from the start. I didn't like her."

"And why is that?"

She sat back as if the question was absurd. "She was just the extra *baggage* that came along with my marriage. Her, that horrid son of hers, and of course, little miss roll-around, the twin on wheels."

"I see," said Grave. No love lost here. "Well, then, do you know why anyone would have wanted to kill your *step*daughter?"

"Other than myself, you mean?" she said, quickly adding, "not that I did."

"Yes, someone else." At least she was being forthright.

"Anyone who dealt with that bitch, *or* watched how Darius pampered her, *or* had to suffer through a house filled with those terrible paintings of red tuna fish."

"Mackerel," said Grave, the voice of Bendigo Bottoms in his head, comparing life to a saltwater finfish of the tribe *Thunnini*, a subgroup of the mackerel family. Was life chunk light or white Albacore? And was bread a factor?

"Mackerel, tuna . . . who cares?"

"Indeed," said Grave. "But do you have anyone specific in mind?"

Philomena reflected briefly, raising her eyes to the ceiling, then quickly down, like the sudden drop of a faulty window. "No, actually, but it's a wonder she lived as long as she did."

This was getting him nowhere. He pressed on. "We were both in this room when we learned about Whitney's death. Where were you before?"

"Before?"

"Yes, your whereabouts, from the time you woke up to the time you entered this room Sunday morning."

Philomena blinked. "To what level of detail?"

"Just the high spots will do."

"Okay, that would be a few minutes in the laboratory, followed by the usual meeting in the dining room with the staff to plan the day, followed by a brief walk across the foyer to this room."

"And I presume by 'staff' you mean the robots?"

"Yes, and Ms. LaFarge."

"Was anyone absent from the meeting?"

Philomena nodded. "Darius, of course. He never attended our meetings. Marilyn, Jimmy, George, and Ms. LaFarge were also absent, but that would not have been unusual. Attendance is always based on availability. If a robot or Ms. LaFarge was on task, they were free to continue on task. If something affected them, we'd track them down and let them know."

"I see. And what was discussed in that meeting?"

"Nothing, as it turns out. No new instructions for the day, so everyone dispersed to perform their default duties."

"And is *that* unusual?"

"No."

This line of questioning had withered on the vine to its ultimate conclusion: he would have four additional interviews, not counting Roy Lynn, assuming Mrs. Hawthorne would permit it.

"Let's talk about Saturday afternoon and evening, *after* I had left, when everyone knew of Ms. Jones's death. Was there any discussion about her murder?"

Philomena seemed puzzled. "How do you mean?"

"You know, just conjecture among the staff about who might have done it?"

"Detective, you seem to be at sea on both murders."

His mind jumped from "sea" to fish to tuna fish, to sandwich, to the meaning of life and its fishy connection. "Please, answer the question."

"Robots don't really talk among themselves, and as for everyone else, I can't say. I certainly didn't discuss the murder with anyone."

"Not even your husband?"

"Ms. Jones was not exactly one of our favorite people, certainly not mine, so the way I looked at it, the less said the better."

"So if you didn't talk about it, what did you do for the rest of the day?"

"Why, my knitting, of course." She lifted the scarf as evidence.

"It's a beautiful scarf. For your husband?"

Philomena appeared pleased, then baffled. "It's my knitting, a scarf, you see. It's not *for* anyone."

Now Grave was baffled. "But why do it, then?"

She held up the scarf again, moving it closer to Grave so he could get a better look. "It's my knitting. It's what I do."

The woman was apparently obsessed with her knitting. "All right, can I ask a *question* about your knitting?"

"Of course. I'm an expert, you see."

"I can see that. Tell me, how many knitting needles do you have?"

Philomena looked as if Grave had asked her to explain string theory. She picked up her needles and showed them to him. "Why, two, of course."

"No, I mean in total."

"Two," she said. "*These.*"

"No others?"

"Detective, I'm sure you know that the process of knitting involves the use of *two* needles to manipulate yarn to create a fabric or textile consisting of a number of interlocking loops."

"Yes, of course, but don't you need different sized needles for different tasks, and wouldn't you naturally acquire a variety of needles over the course of your knitting career?" He was pleased that he had matched the length and complexity of her sentence.

"I only knit scarves like this, so I only need two needles."

"And where do you keep the needles when you're not knitting?"

"In my room, on the dresser, with my *knitting.*"

"So anyone would have access to them?"

"Yes, but no one else knits, so . . ."

He wasn't going to get much further with this line of questioning, either. "If you don't mind, I'd like Dr. Polk to have a look at them."

"The needles?"

"Yes. He's just outside in the foyer. It will only take a minute."

Philomena stood to leave.

"No, I meant after the interview," said Grave.

Philomena sat back down. "You have more questions?"

Grave nodded. He wasn't sure whether now would be the best time to ask, but he did anyway. "Where is your brother, Chester Clink?"

Philomena shrugged, not at all surprised by the question. "I have no idea. Lurking about, or doing whatever serial killers do between kills."

"I thought you were close."

Philomena glanced around as if she were expecting to see her brother standing next to her. She was clearly not as bright as he had thought, or maybe she was just one of those gullible people who seem to take everything literally.

"No," said Grave. "Close in the sense that you have a close relationship with your brother."

"Oh, of course. No, I haven't seen him in years."

"But surely you were close as children."

"As close as brother and sister can be when the brother is locked away in a room all day."

"Ah, yes, the room," said Grave, delighted that the conversation had taken a turn to one of his pressing questions. "Are there any secret passages in the house?"

Philomena snorted. "Not that I could ever find, or for that matter, not that Chester could find. If there were, we would have been dealing with a lot of disemboweled cats and dogs."

"Well, then . . ."

Philomena glanced at her watch. "If that's all, then."

Grave held up a hand. "One thing before you go. Would it be all right if I interviewed Roy Lynn?"

Philomena weighed the question, the scales on each side dipping down, then lifting up several times before sinking one final way. "I couldn't care less, detective."

"You could be present, of course."

The whole idea seemed distasteful to her. "Whatever for?"

"No reason, really," said Grave. "Be sure to show your needles to Dr. Polk on your way out."

Philomena gathered up her knitting as best she could and walked from the room, the scarf trailing along behind her like a tartan snake, Grave also trailing, trying not to step on it.

Smithers watched her leave, then turned to Grave. "Sir, shall I fetch Master Waters?"

"Yes," said Grave, "and Ms. LaFarge if she's available."

Her presence wasn't technically required now that Mrs. Hawthorne had demurred, but it would be good to have someone in the room who knew the young hellion well, particularly if that someone was as beautiful as Ms. LaFarge, a woman who pushed all thoughts of tuna fish sandwiches from his mind. Mostly.

30

Grave paced back and forth in the foyer, trying to collect his thoughts while he waited for the arrival of Ms. LaFarge and Roy Lynn. Polk and his team were nowhere to be seen, although several of their numbered markers were evident throughout the foyer and part way up the stairs. They must have found more than they expected.

The elevator door across the foyer opened and Polk stepped out, his pace quickening when he saw Grave. He stopped abruptly a few steps later, beckoning Grave.

"There you are. Come along, you need to see this."

Grave followed him into the elevator. "What have you got?"

Polk said nothing but tilted his head in a way that suggested Grave would just have to wait and see. The elevator proceeded down, opening to a busy laboratory, Polk's minions in white everywhere, scouring the place.

The floor had even more evidence markers, stretching from one end to the other.

"Looks like you found a lot," said Grave.

"Fingerprints, for one. I'm guessing just about everyone's, but we'll see."

"Any blood?"

"Yes, indeed." He pointed at various markers. "See there, an invisible trail leading from one end of the lab directly into the elevator."

"So she was killed here?"

"It would seem so. Killed here, dragged into the elevator and through the foyer to the stairs."

"How'd you miss that on Saturday?"

Polk bristled. "Because I don't keep all the equipment in the trunk of my car, detective."

"All right, sorry," said Grave, scanning the room once more. "Blood, fingerprints, anything else?"

Polk beamed. "Ah, the prize."

He walked over to a low, stainless-steel cabinet and carefully opened the doors. Inside was a neatly folded pile of what looked like women's clothes, topped by a small purse and a pair of shoes.

"May I?" said Grave.

"Yes, but gloves," said Polk, pulling out a pair of gloves for Grave. "Careful of the purse and shoes. We've already done our fingerprint work, but still, be careful."

Grave took a pen out of his pocket and slipped it under the strap of the little purse, one of those impossibly small purses that women take along to cocktail parties. He'd always wondered what small assortment of things a woman would take along in such a purse. He considered the possibilities, or *purse*abilities.

"May I open it?"

"Be my guest."

Grave undid the little golden clasp and peered inside. A tampon, a lipstick, a tissue, a credit card, and a wrapped lollipop, the kind with a soft center. No money, no cellphone, no keys.

"Odd," Grave said.

"How so?" said Polk.

"No keys."

"Ah," said Polk, peering into the purse, "and no cellphone."

Grave shook his head. "No, she was told not to bring her cellphone to the unveiling event."

"Seriously?" said Polk. "I can't imagine being without my phone, even if I were told to leave it at home. Who would do that?"

Perhaps no one, thought Grave. Perhaps she did have a phone with her and the killer took it, along with her keys.

"The keys!" he blurted out.

"What?"

"The keys, the keys, he must have needed them to get into her car, or her apartment, or her gallery."

"That," said Polk, "or he wanted to keep someone out of those places."

Grave was kicking himself. Captain Morgan had been right—he should have followed up on all three on Saturday.

"Polk, are you about finished here?"

Polk looked around. "Pretty much. Another half hour or so should do it."

Grave glanced at his missing watch, the actual time still not evident. "Good, I'll finish up one more interview, and then we need to check out her apartment and her gallery, and possibly her car, if she has one." He couldn't recall seeing one when he had arrived on Saturday.

"Way ahead of you. We already have a team there."

"Great, but what about a car. When you arrived here on Saturday morning, were there any other cars parked outside?"

Polk reflected a few seconds. "Not that I can recall. Just mine, a few patrol cars, and the CSI van."

"Maybe she took a taxi here."

Polk nodded. "Or one of those new-fangled alternative services, Oozer or Oober, or something."

Grave hoped not. With his luck, she would have taken the driverless kind.

"Or," continued Polk, "she was murdered in her apartment or her gallery, and then transported here."

"I thought you said she was murdered here."

"Most likely, yes, but elsewhere is still a possibility."

Grave nodded. "So, will you join us at her apartment when you're done here?"

"Maybe, it depends what else we find here, and the time. Probably nothing more, and we'll probably wrap up pretty quickly, so yeah, maybe."

"Have I ever told you how much I love your decisiveness?"

31

Every time he saw Ms. LaFarge he thought his life had reached a turning point, a life-changing milestone promising a long, happy life, skipping hand in hand down some bucolic lane accompanied by twittering bluebirds, the sky the bluest of blues, the clouds puffed up like cotton candy, a rainbow arching over all.

And then she would speak.

"What the fuck! Have you no sense of decency? His mother has been dead less than a day, and you want to *interrogate* him?"

Grave gulped, the sound echoing through the foyer and up the stairs, but Ms. LaFarge seemed not to notice.

She was back in uniform this morning, which did nothing to hide her beauty. Say what you will, beauty will out, even in sensible nurse's shoes.

He tried to mollify her. "Actually, it's more like a little friendly *talk*, and I promise, if he or you want to end it—at any time—just say so."

LaFarge snorted. "How about now?"

"Um, no," said Grave, ushering the three of them—Ms. LaFarge, Roy Lynn, and Smithers—into the drawing room.

Roy Lynn, perhaps through grief, perhaps through ennui, had thrown off his Indian Chief costume in favor of a Darth Vader outfit, complete with helmet, cape, and light saber, which he switched on and began swinging as they entered the room. Ms. LaFarge pulled it out of his hand without comment, and guided him into the chair facing Grave.

"Would you mind taking off the mask, young man?" said Grave.

The boy's voice was years away from any hope of reaching the depths of James Earl Jones's voice, but he did his best to mimic it.

"If this is a consular ship, where is the ambassador?" he said, looking around the room. Roy Lynn had apparently retreated to the questionable safety of *Star Wars* quotations.

"Could you just take it off? I'd really like to see your face," said Grave, his attention diverted by Ms. LaFarge, who had just crossed her legs, the quick flash of thigh nearly knocking him off his chair.

"I find your lack of faith disturbing," said Roy Lynn Vader.

"Very well, keep it on." Grave glanced over at Ms. LaFarge again, whose legs remained steadfastly crossed, even as her foot bobbed up and down suggestively. Suggestive of what, he wasn't sure, but a suggestion of some sort, nonetheless.

"I know you've just lost your mother, and I am so sorry for that, but I would like to know your thoughts about both crimes."

Roy Lynn Vader squirmed in his seat, then settled back into character. *"She must have hidden the plans in the escape pod. Send a detachment down to retrieve them. See to it personally, Commander."*

Was there a clue in there? Grave wasn't sure. "Did your mother talk about the death of Ms. Jones, or anything about her, really?"

"I hope so for your sake, Commander. The Emperor is not as forgiving as I am." He ended with one of Vader's signature breathy breaths.

"So, what did Whitney, your mother, say?"

"That name no longer has any meaning for me."

Grave persisted, wondering when Roy Lynn would run out of quotes and answer a question straight on. Grave tried once more.

"I realize this is a troubling time for you, Roy Lynn, but I really could use your help."

"What is thy bidding, my Master?" Roy Lynn's breathy breath was losing steam, as was his attention, his head turning left and right, scanning the room, finally resting on the light saber.

"Ah," said Grave. "Would you like your light saber back?"

Roy Lynn nodded vigorously.

"Then please answer my questions."

Roy Lynn slumped in his chair and crossed his arms. *"You have failed me for the last time, Admiral."*

Now Grave felt like slumping back in his chair. "All right, then, do you have *anything* to say about the murder of your mother? Anything at all?"

Roy Lynn uncrossed his arms and leaned forward in his chair, the gap between them closing. *"Sister!"* he shouted. *"So, you have a twin sister! Obi-Wan was wise to hide her from me. Now his failure is complete. If you will not turn to the dark side, then perhaps she will!"*

"Wait, what?" said Grave, "Are you saying your aunt had something to do with this?" Grave knew she could move, but was she really capable of the effort required to accomplish either murder? He thought not.

"If you only knew the power of the dark side," said Roy Lynn, adding an unnecessary and wholly out of character, "Bwa-ha-ha!"

This was getting him nowhere, or perhaps some somewhere he didn't recognize as a somewhere. He tried a different tack.

"Do you think robots, er, I mean *droids*, were involved?"

Out of the corner of his eye, he could see Smithers suddenly turn his way, then quickly turn back.

Roy Lynn shrugged. *"Don't be too proud of this technological terror you've constructed. The ability to destroy a planet is insignificant next to the power of the Force."*

Grave puffed out his cheeks and threw up his hands, exasperated. "I guess that will be all, Roy Lynn." He turned to Ms. LaFarge. "Unless you can translate all this, I guess we're done."

Ms. LaFarge shook her head and stood, motioning for Roy Lynn to stand. "I don't think so. It's just too soon, detective. He's locked himself away, as you can see."

"Very well." He turned to Roy Lynn. "You can go now, and thank you for your, um, *help*."

Roy Lynn stood, took his light saber from Ms. LaFarge, and began walking toward the door, dragging it behind him, the Force apparently at a low ebb. *"This will be a day long remembered. It has seen the end of Kenobi; it will soon see the end of the Rebellion."*

"We can only hope," said Grave.

The boy stopped as he reached the door and turned to scan the room. *"I sense something. A presence I have not felt since . . ."*

His voice trailed off, and then he was gone. Ms. LaFarge watched him leave, then turned back to Grave. "It was worth a try, I guess."

Grave started to respond, but she was already out the door, her shoes squelching sensibly across the marble floor. He watched her and the boy walk across the foyer. He could have sworn he saw a bluebird hovering over her head. He certainly had more than a few over his.

32

Blunt was beside himself. She could *see* him, she could actually see *him*. More to the point, as she had already remarked in equal wonder, he could see *her*.

Shortly after the confused and puzzled receptionist had accepted the fact that a disembodied voice was speaking to her from across the counter, she had ushered Blunt into a small meeting room off the lobby of the headquarters building of Ramrod Robotics and told him a Ms. Thursday, the company spokesperson, would be joining him shortly.

The building looked like it had been designed by an architect with a fetish for triangles, the whole idea of rectangles seemingly absent wherever you looked. As a result, the meeting room appeared to be lopsided, which may have been the effect desired by the architect when he chose to compose it with a crazed mixture of equilateral, isosceles, and scalene triangles. If you didn't focus hard, the room appeared to be tumbling away from you.

Perhaps it was this assemblage of impossible angles that had revealed Blunt to Ms. Thursday and Ms. Thursday to Blunt, each of them startled by the clear awareness that they were actually being seen by the other person. If their wide-eyed meeting had been part of a comic strip, they would have existed in a panel showing them with the word "Sproing!" in a cartoon bubble over their heads, or "boing," or some other variant of "oing" indicating a level of eye-popping surprise that could only be captured in a cartoon.

They sat there for some minutes, studying each other, each delighted by the delight in the face of the other as they went down a checklist of features to make sure that what they were seeing was actually what they were seeing. Eyes, check. Nose, check. Lips, check, and so on, all the indicators that would identify them as humans and not just amorphous clouds floating in space.

What Blunt saw was a woman so nondescript she was beautiful beyond measure, at least to him. He had certainly seen more beautiful women, but their beauty had been spoiled by a lack of awareness of him. He simply wasn't part of their world when they scanned the room, their eyes vacant, not seeing what was right there in front of them. Ms. Thursday, on the other hand, was so aware of him he felt like a person for the first time, her eyes dancing over his every feature. She could barely contain herself. Nor could he.

After a few minutes of stuttering pleasantries, Ms. Thursday managed to gather herself sufficiently to proceed.

"How might I help you, Sergeant?" *He has the cutest nose!*

Blunt cleared his throat. "Well, ma'am, I'm working on a case involving robots—two murders, I'm afraid—and I'm here to gather information about how robots work." *How did she get her teeth so white?*

"I see," she said. "In that case, I think it would be useful to show you our product gallery." *Oh, his hands!*

She ushered him out of the room and down a long hall of impossible angles that made Blunt think he was walking down a colon constructed by his seventh-grade geometry teacher. At the end was a door marked "Gallery," which she opened by placing her hand in a scanner.

"Why all the security?" *She has the shapeliest neck!*

"Industrial espionage, it's just rampant." *He's taller than I first thought.*

The door swung open to reveal a room seemingly longer than the colon they had just passed through. Various machines and what were obviously robots lined the walls on both sides, with disconcerting gaps necessitated by the obtuse and acute angles of the architect's triangular fixation.

She walked quickly past several of the machines, pointing a

delicate finger at each. "In the early days, we focused on robotic lawnmowers and vacuum cleaners like these. As you can see, they progressed from rather gawky assemblages to the sleek machines of today, like the Turbo Trimmer 9000 here, our top-of-the-line mower. Once the mower has scanned its target lawn, it can mow it at speeds of up to forty miles per hour. Slightly slower in the corners, of course." *I love the way he looks at me.*

"Impressive," said Blunt, "but what I'm really interested in is humanlike robots, like those down there." *Should I ask her about her perfume? It's intoxicating!*

She nodded and escorted him past the other mowers and vacuums, some miniature models in display cases that allowed you to push various buttons and levers to see them in action.

"Here's where our history of simbotics begins," she said. *He walks like John Wayne!*

"Simbotics?" *Those lips!*

"Sorry, it's a trademarked term we're trying to push. A simbot, or simdroid—the terms are synonymous—is an android that perfectly resembles a real person—looks, size, voice, mannerisms, you name it." *He's so cute when he's puzzled.*

"Why go that direction? Why not robots—I mean androids—that are more generic?" *She can raise a single eyebrow!*

"Good question. In fact, we did try that at first, but we soon found that people wanted androids with more personality, droids that were different from those of their neighbors. Generics just didn't cut it in the marketplace." *If he smiles again, I'll just melt!*

"Sounds like the robots, er, droids we're dealing with." *Don't look at her breasts, don't look at her breasts.*

"Something like this?" she said, pointing at one of the droids. "Our Peter O'Toole model?" *He likes my breasts!*

"Yes, exactly that. We're dealing with eleven of them." *Her hair is so golden. Like silk.*

"Wow, really? That's pretty old technology. Which series?" *Is there something wrong with my hair?*

"Um, I'm not sure. What's the difference?" *Have eyes ever been that blue?*

"It depends on the series. Series 2 robots, for example, have slightly more natural skin and a somewhat longer battery life. Fourteen days, as opposed to just seven for the Series 1." *Those shoulders!*

"And Series 3?" *Why the frown?*

"There was no Series 3 in the Peter O'Toole model. The whole series was discontinued, in fact. Replaced, as you can see, by our Singer Series." *Even his knitted brow is cute!*

He looked down the line of robots and instantly recognized Taylor Swift, Justin Timberlake, Beyoncé, and that new singer, whatshername, the one who sings *Bladder Blues*. "Interesting, and why's that?" *She looks worried. Why?*

"Well, hmm, normally I wouldn't say, but since you're the police, you must already know about it. At least I think you do." *Is he angry with me?*

"Perhaps we do, but I certainly don't. Why was the model discontinued?" *Why is she so apprehensive?*

"Two reasons, really. First, and most obvious if you think about it, a lot of people no longer remember Peter O'Toole. I know, I know, how could they *not* know about *Lawrence of Arabia*? But the real reason—and I tell you this in complete confidence—is that we discovered a rather *unfortunate* flaw in the model's simcortex." *He seems to have calmed down a bit. Whew!*

"Simcortex?" *Her neck is flushed. Stress?*

"Ah," she said, walking over to one of the simbots and pushing on its back, a thin metallic shaft popping out that she then pulled from its back, just to the left of its spine, in the general area above where a human heart would be. *Why are his eyes bugging out?*

"That's the simcortex?" *My god, could that be the murder weapon? It looks like a dipstick.*

"Yes, what our engineers laughingly refer to as the digital dipstick. Everything that makes the droid what it is—*everything*—is stored on the simcortex. Programming, memory, and so on." *Why is his mouth open?*

"May I hold it?" *She seems puzzled.*

"Yes, of course, but be careful. Its edges can be very sharp." *He seems fascinated.*

She handed it over. It was very much like the oil-level dipsticks found in cars, a long shaft with a disk part way up to prevent it from being pushed too far into the oil pan, as well as to assure that accurate measures of oil levels could be taken. It was about the same thickness as an icepick, and sharp. A small drop of oil dripped off the end. *Proto oil?*

She watched him as he turned the dipstick this way and that, examining it from every angle. "To me, it's also like a turkey timer," she said. "You know, one of those white plastic thingys that pop out when the turkey is done? Same exact thing happens when this model's battery runs out." *He's not paying the slightest attention to me.*

"When its battery runs out?" he said, finally, carefully handing the simcortex back to her. *She seems relieved about something.*

"Yes," she said, slipping the dipstick back into the robot and snapping it into place, the handle of its shaft disappearing with a click. The disk on the shaft was the same color as the clothing, so once it was in place, it was almost impossible to see.

"Anyway," she continued, "as I said, it will pop out after seven days, or ten to fourteen in the case of the Series 2." *He seems excited. Great!*

"Right, right. And, again, why exactly was the model discontinued? You mentioned something about an unfortunate flaw?" *I love that smile!*

She blushed. "I guess I was being a tad euphemistic. It seems one of the Series 1 droids killed a child on Halloween." *Is that what gob-smacked looks like?*

"Killed? I thought that was impossible. Asimov's Law and all that." *Am I yelling?*

"Yes, *usually*. The thing is, like all the other simdroids in this series, it was programmed to kill various household pests. In this particular case, when a little girl costumed as a spider came to the door, well, um, you see what I mean, it wasn't pretty." *He is so handsome when he's astonished. Like a little boy.*

He took her hands in his, the effect like an electric shock. "This is amazing! And what did Hawthorne do to correct it, the flaw." *Did she feel what I felt?*

"Hawthorne?" *What's he talking about?*

"Hawthorne, your CEO." *She seems mystified.*

"Oh, oh, right, right, Mr. Hawthorne," she said after a long pause. "He was tossed out by the board a while back, before my time, actually. He wanted to proceed with a new model, some sort of custom droid, you know, some sort of design your own robot thing, but the board was having none of it." *Why is his mouth hanging open?*

"So he no longer works here?" *She is so beautiful.*

She shook her head. "No, of course not." *Please tell me he's not going to leave so soon.*

"Ms. Thursday, do you think you could possibly break away from your duties for a few hours to help us with this case?" *She is so quick to smile, and what a smile!*

"Yes, of course!" *Calm down, girl.*

"Wonderful." *I could just hug her!*

He pulled out his cellphone, a wide smile on his face, one that Ms. Thursday would later characterize as "delightful" when she was safely at home on her couch, discussing her day with her cat, Mr. Jinx.

33

The drive from Ramrod Robotics to the mansion took only minutes, but Blunt and Thursday had still managed to cover brief histories of their families. June Thursday was the youngest of three Thursday sisters, the others named April and May. Her father, August, had continued the family's traditional naming scheme, and in June's case it had seemed doubly appropriate since she was actually born in June, on a Thursday. The family celebrated her birthday every year, of course, but even more so in years when her birthday fell on a Thursday in June.

Blunt had explained his family's naming scheme as well, which was based totally on alliteration. So, he was named Barry, his father was named Bixby, and his brothers were named Barnaby, Baxter, and Bart. His mother's name, Charlotte, didn't fit the scheme, of course, but everyone called her Bitsy, so it all worked out.

June laughed when she heard this. "Well, my mom comes close to fitting our naming convention. Her name is Wendy. *Wendy Thursday,* get it?" *Oh, how he loved her laugh.*

They passed a caravan of patrol cars and CSI vans heading out as they came into the mansion's driveway. Apparently, Polk had finished up for the day. The media, on the other hand, was still encamped outside the front door of the mansion, which would be a problem for Detective Grave, but not for Blunt and Thursday, who weren't recognized as actual people until they were almost through the door.

Grave was waiting for them in the foyer and quickly ushered them into the drawing room, not quite sure who was who, one vaguely human-shaped cloud much like another, although the smaller cloud smelled much better.

Blunt quickly cleared things up, his voice coming from the cloud on the right. "This is Ms. June Thursday, the woman I spoke to you about."

Grave turned to the other cloud. "It is so nice to, um, meet you."

The cloud that was June giggled. "Likewise. Happy to help out, if I can."

They went over all that Blunt had learned at Ramrod Robotics, June jumping in from time to time to clarify the fine points of robots, androids, and simdroids, and confirming that the robots did, indeed, use proto oil. Naturally, Grave was interested in that, as well as the simcortex and Hawthorne's departure from Ramrod Robotics.

"I wasn't there at the time," she said, "but apparently it was quite nasty. As I understand it, they even took away his compensation package, so he left with nothing."

"Very interesting," said Grave, "and counter to what we formerly understood, or at least assumed. Well, then, I'll be interviewing Mr. Hawthorne in a few minutes. While I'm doing that, I'd like you two to inspect each of the robots. Polk left behind a technician, who's gathered the robots in the laboratory. He'll need your help to take samples from this dipstick thingy. We're looking for blood, of course, from either or both victims. Ms. Thursday, do you think they'll give us any trouble?"

Thursday shrugged. "I shouldn't think so. Once we pull out their simcortex, they will be totally inactive."

"Good," said Grave, turning to Blunt. "Sergeant, the technician needs to tag and bag each of the dipsticks, and leave all the robots inactive for now."

"But sir," said Smithers from the far side of the room.

Grave had completely forgotten about him. "What is it, Smithers?"

"How shall the family ever cope?"

"That can't be helped, I'm afraid."

"Oh, but I do so hate performing their duties. Gardening is so, so—*dirty.*

"I'm sure we can skip gardening for today, and the whole process won't take all that long. They'll all be back in action by tomorrow."

Smithers seemed satisfied. "Very well, sir."

Grave turned back to Blunt. "So, can you do that?"

"Yes, sir," said Blunt. "What about Smithers here?"

Grave looked over toward the door, where Smithers was still looking uncomfortable, even for a robot. "Leave him for now. I want him active for this interview with Mr. Hawthorne. Then we'll see."

Grave watched as two clouds drifted across the room and floated into the foyer. "Smithers, go fetch Mr. Hawthorne."

34

Officer Wallaby, one of Polk's young CSI techs, stood in front of the line of robots like a drill sergeant about to run his troops through a fitness exercise. He seemed totally surprised by the voices coming from behind him, but once he saw the clouds, he knew one of them must be Sergeant Blunt, if only from his voice.

"This is Ms. Thursday, from Ramrod Robotics. She'll be helping us with the sample collections."

Officer Wallaby nodded in the general direction of the second cloud. "Great, how exactly do we do this?"

"Let's get them into their charging stations," said Ms. Thursday, "so they don't collapse on us when we withdraw the dipsticks."

"Dipsticks?" said Wallaby.

"Don't worry, I'll do it."

Wallaby nodded and started moving the robots one by one into the charging stations, like horses into a starting gate.

"Can you tell anything at this point?" said Blunt.

"They're all Series 1 robots. The simulated hair is the giveaway. Too shiny to be a Series 2 like your Mr. Smithers upstairs."

Wallaby shoved the final robot into its station and turned back to Blunt and Thursday. "Ready to go."

As Wallaby stood next to her with waiting evidence tags and bags, Thursday gingerly removed each simcortex, examining it carefully before dropping it into the waiting bag.

"Interesting," she said as she dropped the last dipstick into an evidence bag. "They look like Series 1 robots, but the simcortex is wrong."

"Wrong?" said Blunt.

"Too advanced, I mean. And by *advanced* I mean well beyond a Series 2 even. It looks somewhat like the ones in our Singer Series, but still quite different. Once your CSI folks finish with them, it would be good to let our engineers have a look. These droids may have capabilities we know nothing about."

"Okay," said Blunt. "Sounds like a plan."

Wallaby had boxed up the samples and was heading for the elevator.

"So, what now, Sergeant?" said Thursday.

Blunt smiled at her. "Detective Grave will want to talk with you further, I'm sure, after he finishes up with Mr. Hawthorne. If I'm not mistaken, we'll find a buffet in the dining room."

Thursday beamed. "Wonderful, the smell of proto oil in the morning makes me hungry."

35

Darius Hawthorne sauntered into the drawing room, his sandals flapping against his heels and the floor in a way that was anything but rhythmic and that pushed the envelope of annoying. He sat down opposite Grave and crossed his long legs, pointing the business end of his foot directly at Grave, who pushed his own chair back a few inches to avoid any contact.

"I want you to know first off how ridiculous this all is," said Hawthorne, "and secondly, that I have requested and received permission from the mayor himself to claim the body of my daughter and lay her to rest."

Grave could feel the blood draining from his face. *The audacity of the man! The cowardice of the mayor! Good god, had Captain Morgan just caved?*

"I see." He could tell his voice was quavering.

"And thirdly, what with all the funeral arrangements—flowers, the obituary, and so forth—I can only give you five minutes for any further questions you may have of me." With that, he slapped his lips together tightly, sat back, and arched his eyebrows to indicate victory.

Grave suppressed the temptation to close the space between them and throttle the man. Instead, he calmed himself using the techniques taught to him by Master Cho, his Hap Wadoo instructor, simultaneously clenching his toes and taking a deep, cleansing breath.

Hap Wadoo was a new form of self-defense program that focused on the four pillars of self-preservation—Deny, Delay, Deflect, and

Depart—all skills promoting flight over fight. As such, the one thing Hap Wadoo wasn't was a martial art. Indeed, it was the latest trendy new thing, one of a burgeoning field of alternative programs known as the *partial* arts, which featured colorful achievement belts that could be earned without the burden of effort, discipline, or dedication. Needless to say, it was sweeping the country without the effort required by a broom.

"Mr. Hawthorne, before you proceed to some inappropriate 'fourthly,' let me assure you that this little conversation of ours will last *as bloody long as I want it to last!*" The thing about Hap Wadoo techniques is that as effective as they are, their effectiveness is brief and transient and unsustainable through a long sentence.

Hawthorne took it all in stride, sneering back at him and raising his hand, his eyebrows dancing with mocking delight that Grave had once again slipped into a British accent.

"Mr. Hawthorne," Grave shot back, "why have you been lying to me?"

Hawthorne shrugged and lowered his hand. "Whatever do you mean?"

Grave tested the limits of Hap Wadoo once more. "You said you were the CEO of Ramrod Robotics. We know now that you are *not.*"

"I said nothing of the kind, detective. If memory serves, I said that you might *remember* me as the CEO of Ramrod Robotics. Past tense, you see."

One of the basic tenets of Hap Wadoo is to ignore or deflect the blows of your opponent. Several techniques are employed, most notably, the "dampening bell technique." Using this technique, when your opponent strikes a blow, you first imagine him striking a bell instead of you, the size and tone of the bell determined by the severity of the blow, a rather weak blow creating a tinkle in your mind, a strong blow creating a dinner bell in your mind, and a severe blow creating the bells of Notre Dame in your mind. With each blow, you imagine grasping the bell with both hands, dampening its sound and intensity. Or, as Master Cho was wont to say, *control the clapper*. Of course, this technique only works while you remain conscious.

Grave thus took the blow in stride, and parried with his own blow. "You *also* lied about the capabilities of your robots, particularly as those capabilities relate to killing."

Hawthorne remained calmly obstinate. "I said no such thing, detective.

"Did too!"

"Did not."

This schoolyard exchange went on for some seconds, Grave heated, Hawthorne cool, until Grave was able to break away, the voice of Master Cho echoing in his head: *Taunt not. Heavy fists, not hot air.*

"We know, Mr. Hawthorne—*know*—that the reason you were let go at Ramrod was that one of your robots killed a young girl on Halloween, thinking her a spider."

The blow seemed to have hit home, at least briefly, Hawthorne quickly regaining his composure. "It wasn't *fair*. Something like that was just a *freak* occurrence."

"It appeared your directors disagreed. Perhaps they thought the possibility of large spiders and other animals and pests was all too common, particularly on Halloween."

"Damn them!" said Hawthorne, although not forceful enough to require an exclamation point. The change in his voice was merely an increase in volume—cool words said loudly. "Damn them to hell! I was on the verge of a major breakthrough, and they *knew* it."

"Custom robots, you mean?"

"Yes, exactly. It would have been a whole new world. Just imagine it, detective, a world where you could design a robot to suit your every requirement."

"You mean like butler, mechanic, and so on?"

"No, no, not just servants, but *friends, loved ones*—replicas, if you will, robotic clones."

"What?"

"With the same personality, intelligence, and most of all, *independence*."

"What, like free-range robots?"

Hawthorne gave him a blank, withering look, if that's possible, and apparently it was for Hawthorne. "Don't make light of it, detective. Imagine, say, you lost a loved one. If the directors had just given me a little more time, I could have made it possible to create a replacement for the lost loved one, accurate in every detail:

appearance, mannerisms, memories, everything." He slumped back in his chair and stared at his foot, which continued to invade the space of Detective Grave.

"You realize," said Grave, "that these lies move you up on our list of suspects."

Hawthorne woke up as if from a deep sleep. "What? What are you saying? You can't possibly think I had anything to do with those murders. What, kill my own daughter? Ridiculous. And when are you going to accept the fact that I was *locked* in that room, that I couldn't *possibly* have killed Ms. Jones?"

Grave was in no mood to let him off the hook, even though he had not worked out the details of the crime. "But you were among the last to see your daughter, weren't you? You and Smithers were alone with her in the studio, trying to talk her down from her tantrum about the fish."

"But apparently not *the* last, detective. And she was my *daughter.*"

Cruelty was not part of the Hap Wadoo tradition, but Grave wanted to see how Hawthorne would react, anyway. "A daughter with more issues than you cared to deal with. A daughter with tendencies you disliked. In short, a daughter that you thought to replace with a better daughter, a robotic daughter."

Hawthorne had been shaking his head the whole time. "How dare you! I loved my daughter, *loved* her!"

There was something disingenuous about his tone. The words themselves could have been quite dramatic, but the delivery lacked the intensity you would expect. If he had been auditioning for the part of Mr. Hawthorne, the casting director would have undoubtedly said, "Next!"

Hawthorne stood and marched from the room as if a casting director had said just that, slamming the door behind him.

"Will that be all, then?" said Smithers from across the room.

As with most of the interviews, Grave had forgotten Smithers was even there. "Do you think he's telling the truth?"

Smithers cocked his head. "Truth? Objective or subjective?"

"What?"

"Truth, sir, can be objective or subjective, and all the shades in between, the first being what is fact for all observers, regardless of perspective, the second being information sorted to suggest fact from the perspective of one or more observers, a lesser part of the universe of observers, for the purpose of deception or advantage."

"I love it when you talk dirty, Smithers."

"What?"

"Nothing. Let's go with *objective* truth."

Smithers hummed a few seconds. "Yes and no, sir. He was a bit in the weeds when it came to what is robotically possible. He knows, in fact, that he has already developed the ability to create a custom robot. Is working on one now, in fact."

"You mean the one that's, um, anatomically correct, so to speak?"

"No, not Dick, the sexbot. Something completely other."

Grave was stunned. "Really? What kind of custom robot? Or rather who?"

"I'm not sure. I saw it some weeks ago, when it was far from completion. Mr. Hawthorne was unhappy that I had seen it, and covered it up with a sheet."

"But there's nothing like that in the laboratory now," mused Grave.

"No, sir."

"And what about Whitney's tantrum? You were there. What happened?"

Smithers paused briefly, apparently sorting his memory files. "She was distraught, bordering on maniacal. Mr. Hawthorne tried to calm her with soothing words, but she lashed out at him with part of a broken picture frame."

"And she cut him?"

"Yes."

"Go on, go on."

"He grabbed his hand. She stumbled back, trying to distance herself from him, screaming for him to get out. I started toward him, to help with his hand, but he told me to leave the room."

"Leave?"

"Yes, so I turned and walked to the door." He paused, his head turning left, then right, then up, then down.

"What is it, Smithers?"

"A sequence anomaly, sir."

"A what?"

"A gap in my memory. Sir, I never opened the door. I was just suddenly out of the room, heading down the stairs with Mr. Hawthorne."

Grave was sure that Hap Wadoo had something to say about such a revelation, but he was more interested in what Ms. Thursday would have to say.

He rushed from the room, Smithers trailing behind at a much slower pace.

36

Grave was unsure how best to proceed. On the one hand, everything seemed to suggest that Hawthorne was the killer, at least of his daughter. Arresting him now would prevent flight. On the other hand, a gap in a robot's memory might not hold up in court, let alone keep the man in custody. It might be better to let him stay free for now, while they tried to gather additional evidence and determine whether Hawthorne was linked to the murder of Ms. Jones. Perhaps there were clues at her apartment or her gallery that would more directly link Hawthorne to that murder as well.

All these thoughts raced through Grave's mind as he made his way toward the animated voices of Blunt and Ms. Thursday coming from the dining room. He pushed open the door, and stood stock still in wonder.

The foyer was grand, the library sublime, the drawing room posh, the studio full of fish paintings, but this, this dining room, was a feast for the eyes, from the gleaming rosewood table that stretched to tomorrow, to the crystal chandelier that illuminated the room with the light of a thousand thousand twinkling bulbs, to the gleaming buffet along the wall, to the mélange of aromas that filled the room: bacon, burnt toast, hash brown potatoes, eggs, sausages, scrapple, cheese grits, honey ham, roast beef, platter after platter of lunchmeats and cheeses, and urn after urn of coffee. It was enough to divert any hungry man from his task.

But not Grave, a man who had earned his puce belt in Hap

Wadoo, one belt up from beginner's white, a feat that required suppression of desire for a belt-test minimum of fifteen seconds. Thus suppressed, though drooling, he continued into the room, grabbing a chair opposite the blurred images of Sergeant Blunt and Ms. Thursday, and sitting down, completely in control, although shaking noticeably from the rigors of suppression, the smell of bacon testing him dearly. Smithers came up and stood behind Grave's chair, trying to make sense of the second cloud across the table.

"I think we've found our man," Grave said, trying to tear his eyes away from the heaping plates of food in front of them.

"Hawthorne, is it?" said Blunt, crunching on a strip of bacon.

Grave was startled. "Yes, how did you—"

Blunt shrugged. "You just came from interviewing him."

"Oh, right."

"Shall we arrest him, then?"

"Not quite yet. I think I can tie him to his daughter's murder, but I don't have enough evidence yet. I really want us to check out Ms. Jones's apartment and gallery. I just have this sense that we're missing something, particularly about the murder of Ms. Jones."

"Ready when you are, sir," said Blunt, popping a sausage into his mouth, which disappeared into a briefly opening maw at the top of the cloud that was Blunt.

Grave wondered briefly whether he would lose his puce belt status if he had just one little strip of bacon, but he resisted, pushing well past fifteen seconds.

"First, though, I would like to take advantage of your knowledge, Ms. Thursday."

"Certainly, detective."

"Smithers here says he experienced—what was it again, Smithers?"

"A sequence anomaly, sir, a gap in my memory."

"Ah," said Thursday, "I'm not totally up to speed on all the technical mumbo-jumbo. I'm a spokesperson, you see, but I am familiar with that term. That can happen in only two ways, the battery runs out or someone temporarily deactivates or removes the simcortex."

"They call it the digital dipstick, sir," said Blunt, slathering marmalade on a piece of toast floating in front of him. Grave had to look away or risk his puce belt entirely.

"Let me demonstrate," said Thursday, moving around the table. "You'll need to stand up, detective."

Grave stood and watched as Ms. Thursday pressed a spot on Smithers' back, the shaft of the simcortex popping out enough for her to grasp it and pull it slowly out. Smithers slumped, Thursday steadying him enough to move him into a chair.

"My god!" said Grave. "Our murder weapon!"

"Yes, sir," said Blunt. "I thought you'd like that."

"So our killer was working with a robot, perhaps Smithers here, or at least took advantage of his proximity long enough to commit the murder."

"I'm not a detective, but that makes sense to me," said Thursday. She started to put the simcortex back into Smithers.

"No, wait," said Grave. "If we're right, that dipstick thingy will have traces of Whitney's blood, which would be more than enough to tie Hawthorne to the crime."

Blunt was well ahead of him, whipping out an evidence bag and carefully slipping the dipstick into it. "The CSI tech is gone, sir, but I can run this over to the lab on my way to the Jones place. Do we know where that is, sir?"

"Yes, Smithers gave me the address earlier this morning." He pulled out a piece of paper from his suit jacket. "37 Main Street. Apparently, the apartment is over the gallery. I'll meet you there."

"All right, sir, we'll be on our way."

"Wait," said Thursday. "I think I can be of even more help."

"How so?" said Grave.

Thursday smiled in a way that suggested cats and canaries, although the expression went unnoticed by Grave. "The robots. Each simcortex is a recording device. We only have to view what each of the robots has recorded over the past few days."

"And we'll have our robot," said Blunt.

"And perhaps our killer, or *killers*," said Grave.

"Shall we ring Captain Morgan, sir? He'll want to know all this."

Grave wasn't sure whether a puce belt in Hap Wadoo would have the self-control to avoid screaming at Captain Morgan right about now. "No, let's stick to the plan. We can brief him in the morning, when we know more."

"Yes, sir," said Blunt. "We'll be on our way, then."

Grave watched as the clouds floated toward the door. "And sit on Polk if you have to. We need the blood work done right away, so we can review the memory banks of all those dipsticks."

"Right." Blunt and Ms. Thursday drifted through the door and out of the room, two clouds on a mission.

Grave wondered what, if anything, his father could possibly add to what they already knew, but that would have to wait until this evening. He grabbed a handful of bacon and headed for the door. If he was going to survive the gauntlet of news people, especially Claire Fairly, he would need sustenance, puce belt be damned.

37

If anything, the media was in even more of a frenzy when Grave raced down the steps, a thousand microphones in his face, packs of cameras pursuing him like wolves on the hunt, and Claire Fairly, orange as an orange in her TV makeup, in fervent pursuit but losing ground as her high heels sank into the gravel.

He leaped over the door of the Sprite, slid into the seat, and slipped his key into the ignition. The car started up with that same sucking sound, the death rattle, and gospel music filled the air.

Claire Fairly was on him, thrusting her microphone under his chin as he put the car in gear. "Detective," she shouted, "any news, any news at all?"

Grave took a piece of bacon out of his suit pocket and shoved it into her mouth. Her expression changed from surprise to wonder as the bacon did its work.

"Detective," she mumbled as she chewed, forgetting her question entirely. "*Fuck,* that's good!"

Grave sped away, accelerating down the drive, stopping only briefly at the gate to make the turn and speed toward the downtown shopping district, speed being a relative term in an Austin Healey Sprite. The gospel music stopped on a high note for the Lord, and the voice of Reverend Bendigo Bottoms rang out, warning of the dangers of accepting gifts.

"The Eleventh Commandment today is, 'Thou shalt not accept gifts of money, goods, or services in excess of twenty-five dollars in the conduct of thy business.'" Friends, don't be caught in the trap of pay-to-play. Remember what the man said about Greeks bearin' gifts. And don't stop at Greeks. The Devil takes many forms, his evil to perform. Oh, yes he does. No, sinners, the only influence in your life should be the Lord, and in that regard, this commandment shall not apply, tithes and donations of any size gratefully accepted for the furtherance of the Lord's work. Oh, I know what you're thinking. I know you well, sinners. You're thinking, Reverend, is this not a pay-to-*pray* scheme? Wipe that thought from your devious mind and come into the arms of the Lord, who is ready to embrace you and forgive all sins for donations of any amount, although we do have a five-dollar minimum for credit card donations. Drop by the Chapel of Everlasting Forgiveness today, three doors down from the Skunk 'n Donuts on Main Street, or call us at 666-PRAY, Monday through Friday, 8:30 to 5:00. Angels are standing by to take your call."

Gospel music filled the air once more as Grave continued on toward downtown, the density of homes becoming ever thicker as he approached Main Street and the town's three-block long shopping district of two-story buildings, many of which featured shops on the lower level and apartments on the upper level. Flags hung from every lamppost, announcing the town's major annual event, *Crabapalooza*, an event that brought crowds from near and far for all things crab. Grave never missed it, his favorite part the amazing crab race.

His destination was easy to spot, the lights of patrol cars serving as a beacon. He pulled up behind a CSI van and climbed out of the car.

Officers were stringing crime scene tape, blocking off a section of the sidewalk in front of the Epiphany Gallery, which was glittering with broken glass, each shard sparkling red, then blue, then white as the patrol car lights pulsed through their law-and-order sequence.

Grave got the attention of the nearest officer. "Where's Polk?"

The officer shrugged. "Back at the morgue, I guess."

No body, no Polk. "Who's in charge, then?"

"Connors, inside. Mind the glass, detective."

Grave looked at the broken front door. "Did you have to break in like that?"

"Didn't. He did." The officer pointed at a man in the back seat of one of the patrol cars. Grave knew immediately who it was: Calamity Jones.

Grave walked over, opened the door to the patrol car, and got in, forcing Cal Jones to make room. "I don't suppose you have a good excuse for breaking into the gallery."

Jones smirked. "The best excuse, detective. The place is mine now. No crime here, you see, just a grave misunderstanding is all."

Grave conceded the point. Technically, Cal had committed a crime—the gallery was not yet legally his. But technically, he would in fact inherit the gallery, so he had a point. Technically, though, the gallery and apartment were rented, so he had in fact committed a crime against the landlord. But technically, the DA didn't take on cases that were technically based on technicalities.

Grave pressed on. "How long have you been here, inside I mean?"

"Not long. Just long enough to open some windows upstairs. It smells like a dead rat in there."

Grave looked down at Jones's handcuffed hands. "Let's get you out of those. I want you to walk me through everywhere you went and everything you touched while you were inside."

38

Calamity Jones had tried his best to open the door without smashing it, but in the end, a nearby brick had done the trick. Once inside, he had deactivated the alarm system—too late, as it turned out—and walked briefly through the gallery, shaking his head at what people considered art these days, including a stack of hideous fish paintings in a backroom storage area. Then he had climbed the stairs to his sister's apartment, where the smell had grown stronger. As far as he knew, the only thing he'd touched before the police arrived was the window latches and frames.

"You're sure about that?" said Grave.

"Yes, absolutely."

Grave looked around the apartment. He hated this part of the job—going through the possessions of the dead. It just felt wrong to him, ghoulish even.

He could imagine her leaving for the last time, putting her coffee cup into the sink, tossing one scarf aside in favor of another, leaving a stack of mail scattered on her coffee table, making sure the cat's water bowl was full.

She had left a suitcase half packed on the bed, which was strewn with clothing, some for winter, and some for summer. A stack of travel brochures on the coffee table indicated a long trip to multiple locations, and an odd assortment at that: Iceland, Bolivia, Ecuador, Cuba, and Nicaragua. He searched for plane tickets and boarding passes, but found nothing.

More important, he found no evidence of a struggle. She had definitely not been murdered here. On the other hand, they did find her cellphone and keys, indicating that someone had returned to the apartment after the murder, although again, there was no evidence that anything had been disturbed. If the murderer had returned to retrieve something, it must have been in full view or at least easy to find.

There was no car key on the key ring, so there was either no car to find or the murderer had taken just the one key, which made no sense to Grave. She probably didn't own one, so Grave instructed Connor to have one of his men run a check of local taxis and transport services to see when and how she had managed to get to the mansion. They needed to check her phone records as well, and do a full search for DNA evidence. And to be on the safe side, they needed to check the DMV database to see if Ms. Jones actually did own a car. Connor already had several men canvassing the other shops to see if anyone had seen anything suspicious.

As he mulled over everything he had seen and learned so far, Grave had a sudden thought: *Cat?*

He turned to Sergeant Connor, who had followed them throughout the house, making notes on everything that Jones had said. "Where's the cat?"

They searched the gallery: nothing. They searched the apartment, looking under the bed and behind the sofa, the refrigerator, and the washing machine: nothing. And then one of Connors' men gave a shout: "Here!"

He had opened a broom closet in the kitchen, which contained not a single broom. Instead, what they saw was a safe and the cat atop it, a putrescent hand in its mouth. The cat immediately dropped the hand, snarled, and darted out of the closet to its water bowl, where it lapped greedily.

Connor instructed one of his men to bag the hand, but Grave stepped in. "No, not yet, Connor."

He carefully picked up the hand. "It's a modern safe, at least. Opens when the owner's fingers are pressed against these grooves."

He pressed the hand against the grooves, a foul-smelling liquid, part blood, part pus, part who knows what oozing out of the wrist and dripping onto the floor. Grave held his breath, and after a number of attempts, there was an audible click and the safe popped open. Grave had expected to find it empty—the murderer had clearly come back to retrieve whatever was in the safe—but he was wrong. He swung the door open and there it was: The MacGuffin Trophy.

Somewhere, a cat meowed.

39

There is a point in every investigation where you think you are closing in on the killer, where you think you have a complete understanding of what happened, only to be presented with a puzzle piece that stares back at you like a fly in the ointment, a wrench in the works, a stone in one's path, a turd in the pool, a witch in the wardrobe, a hair on the lollipop, a ghost in the machine, or a skunk in the donuts.

Grave was not sure that "skunk in the donuts" was an actual thing, but the whole case stank right about now, and he was hungry besides, so he was more than willing to consider it a valid idiom.

Whatever the idiom, Grave was faced with the fact—if facts even entered into it—that Ms. Jones had somehow managed to steal the trophy from a locked room without being noticed by the other suspects, and then, after locking her prize away in her safe, had inexplicably returned to the mansion to be murdered and unhanded, her hand transported back to the apartment for no apparent reason, after being stolen from the morgue.

Unless, thought Grave, *unless the murderer put the trophy in the safe. But why? And having done that, why leave the hand behind? And for that matter, why steal the trophy in the first place, if you were just going to kill a woman, lop off her hand, and hide the trophy away in the woman's safe?*

In short, nothing made sense as he pulled into his father's driveway and turned off the ignition, the car's engine "running on" for some seconds before agreeing to follow the ignition's clear instructions to stop. His father had warned him about this, told him to look out for it, but Grave hadn't understood a single word and had tuned out his father's salient soliloquy on dieseling, air-fuel ratios, and the evil of oil-burning. All he knew was that he best not mention it, on fear of death.

He got out of the car, walked up the steps, and started to knock, his father's voice yelling out, "It's open!"

Grave walked in, and froze. The day had already been filled with enough surprises to fill a lifetime, but the spectacle of his father standing in front of a whiteboard filled with notes, diagrams, and gruesome photos of the dead certainly topped them all.

"Come see, come see," said his father. The feeble man in the recliner had been replaced by an upright, energized man in a suit and tie, his head topped by the fedora he had earned by making his first collar when he was an up and coming detective in Atlanta many years ago.

Grave approached, apprehensive. He had seen his father like this before, a man obsessed with finding and arresting his nemesis, Chester Clink, serial killer extraordinaire, still lurking. His father had spent much of his career pursuing the man, and now, even in retirement, couldn't let go.

"Don't worry, son, I'm not going to bore you with a recap of every damn murder this man has done. No, just the last two. Look at this."

His father pointed at two photographs, each showing a woman with multiple stab wounds. "Do you see it?"

Grave looked at one photograph, then the other. "Dead women with roses in their mouths. How did you get these?"

His father groaned. "I still have friends, Simon, but forget the roses—yes, they're a significant change in his death tableaus—but look closer."

Grave looked at each photograph again. "Okay, if I'm counting right, each was stabbed in the torso twenty-one times."

"Yes, yes, that's his signature number, of course, but that's not what I'm talking about." He motioned for Grave to look again, but Grave saw nothing.

His father sighed heavily. "Son, there are times when I wonder how you ever became a detective. Here, let me help you."

His father picked up a pencil and pointed at one of the wounds in one of the photos. "Here, look at this wound. Nice and deep, the clear work of a Bowie knife."

"Yes, so?"

"Now look at this wound." He pointed at a wound in the other photograph.

"So?" Grave didn't know what his father was talking about.

"You are a dense one. If you look closely, you'll find that the wound on this woman is *identical* to the wound on the other woman. The exact same cut in the exact same place. What's more, pick any wound and you'll find they're identical on both women. It's like the wounds were done by a machine."

"Or a robot," said Grave.

Now there really was a skunk in the donuts.

40

The moon hung in the sky like a fizzy headache tablet as Grave drove to the precinct the next morning. He wanted to arrive early and gather his thoughts before his meeting with Sergeant Blunt and Captain Morgan. His hangover wasn't helping in the least.

He had spent the previous evening at home, going over the case in his mind, sipping Duct Tape Chardonnay as he reviewed what he knew and didn't know. But the wine that was supposed to fix anything had fixed nothing. By the third glass, in fact, all he was thinking about was Lola LaFarge. And by the fourth glass, all he was thinking about was Lola LaFarge in various positions only Olympic gymnasts could achieve.

And now, in the early hours before dawn, all he was thinking about was a comfortable pillow for his head, which was throbbing to the beat of his 120-decibel gospel choir, a sound that seemed to shake the leaves of the trees as he pulled into the parking lot of the police station and turned off the engine, which once again rattled on for some seconds before dying with a wheeze. He really needed to get some noise-cancelling headphones.

Much to his surprise, Blunt and Morgan were already at their desks, sipping coffee and eating donuts. Grave glanced at the coffee pot, which continued to be empty, and the open box of donuts, which continued to be chocolate-donut-free. He picked up a cinnamon donut, took a bite, and let the cinnamon and sugar fizz on his tongue. It wasn't chocolate, but it would have to do. He thought to take a second bite, but Captain Morgan was already waving his hand, beckoning him. The cloud that was Sergeant Blunt, freshly coated with powdered sugar, walked along with him to the fishbowl. There seemed to be a confidence in his step that completely overwhelmed the flapping of his clown shoes.

Captain Morgan sat behind his desk, rocking back and forth in his chair in the satisfied way any man would rock having just finished the last chocolate donut in the box, a telltale blob of chocolate clinging to his moustache.

Grave had thought to open with a heated complaint about the release of Whitney's body, but Captain Morgan sensed that immediately and beat him to it.

"I know you have every reason to be upset about our releasing the body, Grave, but it was out of my hands. The mayor will be the mayor, goddammit, and besides, Polk said he could deal with it without hurting the case."

As Captain Morgan spoke, Grave watched the blob of chocolate work its way down the length of Morgan's moustache and drop onto his ample belly. Morgan noticed it, too, and deftly scooped it up and popped it into his mouth. "Anyway," he said sheepishly, "the funeral is tomorrow, and I'd like all three of us to attend."

"What?" said Grave, incredulous.

"As a show of respect."

"Respect?" If there was something beyond incredulous, Grave was on a fast track to get there.

Morgan blustered. "All right, Grave, because we've been fuckin' *ordered* to attend, okay?"

"Perhaps the killer will attend as well," offered Blunt, trying to calm down both of them. "We could set up some cameras, film the—"

"Killer, shmiller," interrupted Grave. "I think we *know* who the killer is, or at least we have a pretty good idea."

"Oh, who?" said Morgan.

"None other than Mr. Darius Hawthorne himself."

Captain Morgan's eyebrows rose to their highest possible position. How could he possibly explain such a thing to the mayor? "Explain."

Grave and Blunt took turns telling Captain Morgan all that had happened and been learned on the previous day, from simcortexes and sequence anomalies, to the discovery of The MacGuffin Trophy and the missing hand, to his father's speculation that there was a robotic Chester Clink on the loose, with Chester himself possibly behind *all* the murders.

"And she could actually *see* you, Blunt?" The captain had been more amazed by this discovery than any other.

"Yes, sir, it was quite startling—and wonderful! When she smiles it's as if she invented happiness. When she sneezes—oh, captain, when she sneezes—it is so soft, so feminine, you would swear she had just squeaked out the word *eschew*."

Grave cleared his throat loudly and tried to bring them back to the murders. "So, on the face of it, Hawthorne seems to be our man, at least for the murder of his daughter. The no doubt bloody simcortex, the sequence anomaly, it all seems to fit."

Captain Morgan scratched his head. "But what about this Chester Clink involvement, and how could Hawthorne possibly have done the first murder if he was locked in that damn room? In fact, how does *any* of what you've told me make any sense at all?"

Grave didn't have a good answer, and was about to say so, when Blunt jumped in. "I think we should ignore all that for now. It's like the center pieces of a jigsaw puzzle. You can't make any sense of them until you've locked down the corners and the borders."

Grave and Morgan looked at Blunt in conditional awe, waiting for more than an apt analogy.

Blunt pressed on. "We should have a reading on the blood evidence from the Smithers simcortex this morning, if any, at least blood typing, and June—I mean Ms. Thursday—will be helping us review the simcortex video files on all the robots as soon as we're done here. With any luck, we could have all the answers by the end of the day."

Captain Morgan slapped the top of the desk. "Well, get to it, then!"

Grave and Blunt rose to leave, but Morgan wasn't finished.

"Wait, what about that trophy?"

"Oh, right," said Blunt. "The CSI folks dropped it off here late yesterday evening. They'd finished up with the fingerprinting and whatnot."

"So it's in the evidence locker?" said Morgan.

"Um, no sir."

"Then where is it?" asked Grave.

Blunt pulled a card out of his pocket and glanced down at it. "A Mr. Grant Horatio Thorpe from the Yacht Club picked it up. Said it was the property of the club and its return had been overdue. It seemed on the up-and-up, so I released the trophy to him."

Grave and Morgan both looked down at the floor, a rather useless technique for controlling a person's disappointment and anger with the release of a multimillion dollar trophy to a man who just walked into the station with a business card.

"Blunt, the trophy is *evidence* in this case. We can't just *release* it."

Blunt was mortified. "Yes, sir, I should have—"

"Known better," said Captain Morgan.

"Let me have the card, Blunt," said Grave. He looked at the address, which definitely indicated a location suitably near a large body of water. "It's not that far from here. Let's swing by there and pick it up."

"No," said Captain Morgan. "You two head out to Ramrod Robotics. "I'll have someone pick it up and bring it back here. Of course, the chain of evidence is compromised, so I'm not sure how this will play in court."

"Yes, sir, sorry, sir," said Blunt, a contrite cloud backing toward the door.

Grave shared an arched-brow look with Captain Morgan and handed him the business card. "He's a bit distracted," whispered Grave, "if you know what I mean."

Captain Morgan nodded and whispered back. "You think? See what you can do to get him tracted again."

Grave wasn't sure if *tracted* was even a word, but he wasn't about to issue a Scrabble challenge right about now. Instead, he followed Blunt's lead and backed toward the door, turning as he reached it, accelerating through the station and out the front door.

Sergeant Blunt was standing on the sidewalk, looking miserable, his shadow long in the early morning light, looking like it was trying to escape.

41

The last thing Grave wanted was to listen to endless apologies from Sergeant Blunt, so instead of taking a patrol car, Grave helped Blunt slide into the passenger seat of the Sprite, which was not an easy feat given the man's size, and took some doing.

Once they were underway, the high-decibel gospel choir did the rest, its choral force field completely blocking all other sounds. If Blunt was talking, Grave certainly couldn't hear him. They drove on, the sound enveloping them. And what a glorious sound! In the time he had owned the car, Grave had come to enjoy not just the gospel music, but the deafening sound the broken radio provided, which had a calming effect on him, allowing him to reach a near Zen state as he ran stop signs and traffic lights, lost in his thoughts.

Blunt's puzzle analogy had been apt indeed. They had a thousand puzzle pieces to consider, some with blurry edges, some with edges that shifted and changed shape when you looked at them, some that were clear and sharp but seemingly unrelated to any other pieces, and some, Grave feared, that had fallen off the card table and rolled under the sofa, leaving gaps in the picture.

The voice of Reverend Bendigo Bottoms broke him away from his Zen state, which had taken him from the precinct to the gates of Ramrod Robotics, its headquarters building looming ahead of them, looking like a mountain of discarded triangles.

"The wages of sin is death, so sayeth the Lord. Now, I know some of you don't believe this. I also know some of you would challenge the

Lord's concept of subject-verb agreement. Oh, yes you would. But the point is, when you're sinnin', you're workin' for the Devil himself, and your wages are or is not just death, but the loss of your everlasting soul. That's right, that's right."

Grave pulled into a parking spot and sat there for some minutes, hoping that the reverend would return to a discussion of how life was like a tuna fish sandwich, but he was on a rant against the Devil this morning and was apparently not interested in sandwiches of any kind.

Grave turned off the engine, which stopped immediately, without even a hint of running on. He turned to look at Sergeant Blunt, who was bug-eyed, his blurry lips moving rapidly, if soundlessly, the advantage of hearing returning slowly to each of them.

"Oh, my god!" shouted Blunt, finally audible. "Did you not *see* the stop signs or the traffic lights?" He began to hyperventilate.

"Not to worry," said Grave, patting him on the shoulder. "It's a Zen thing. No harm, no foul."

They climbed out of the car, Blunt requiring the assistance of Grave, who acted as shoehorn, extracting the man from the car with some effort. Once free, they headed up the front steps of the building, where a cloud somewhat smaller than Blunt, and pleasantly perfumed, was waiting.

"Welcome to Ramrod, Detective Grave," said the cloud.

Grave looked around, trying his best to make sense of the building, the sun glinting off its triangular surfaces in different ways and at strange angles, making the building appear to writhe in the sunlight. The whole thing made Grave wish that he had paid more attention to his lessons in solid geometry. He knew there must be a name for this misbegotten shape.

"Good morning, Ms. Thursday," said Grave, noticing that Blunt had moved very close to her.

"June," said Blunt, his voice low and disconcertingly sexual.

"Barry," said June, her tone matching his.

Grave cleared his throat loudly. "Um, can we get on with this, then?"

The clouds separated, the smallest waving her arm, motioning them to the front door. "This way, detective."

Once inside and beyond the curious stares of the receptionist, Thursday led them down a long hallway, Grave barely able to keep his balance as he made his way along, the triangles refusing to let him focus.

Thursday noticed him having difficulty. "Try to focus on the end of the hallway."

"You'll get used to it, sir," said Blunt. "Only takes a minute or so."

"Who designed this?" said Grave.

"I can never remember his name," said Thursday, "but if you google 'angular dissonance,' his name will pop up."

She showed them into a small room, a video studio of some sort, with a large control panel facing a wall filled with monitors, only one of which was on.

"Have a seat, detectives," said Thursday. "I've downloaded and queued up the files from the eleven simdroids. There's a lot to go over, so how would you like to proceed?"

Grave didn't respond. As distracted as Blunt was by Thursday, Grave was even more distracted by what he saw on a side table: a full coffee pot and a large box of donuts, every one of them chocolate.

Thursday followed his eyes. "Ah," she said, "I've managed some coffee and donuts for us. I hope you like chocolate."

Grave didn't need further coaxing, scooping up a donut and gobbling it down as he poured himself a tall cup of coffee.

"So," said Thursday, "how would you like to begin?"

Grave smiled at her. "I'd like to begin with another donut. And then I'd like to see what Smithers was up to in Whitney's studio."

"On Friday or Sunday, sir?" said Blunt.

"Let's start with Sunday. How does this machine work? Can we queue it up?"

Thursday fumbled with a few nobs and threw a few toggle switches and a video of the drawing room came up.

"No, fast forward it a bit," said Grave.

The monitor showed a view of the long staircase, then the open door of the studio, where Whitney was throwing and tearing paintings, all the while screaming incoherently at Mr. Hawthorne, who was obviously trying to calm her.

"There, slow it down."

Thursday hit a button and the video stopped. She hit another and the video started again, at normal speed. Whitney was striking out at Hawthorne with part of a picture frame, hitting his hand hard. Hawthorne had immediately covered the wound with his other hand as Whitney backed into a corner. She looked terrified. Hawthorne turned and walked toward Smithers, shouting something. Then the video had jumped to a view of the staircase and the back of Hawthorne, who was descending the stairs, clutching at his hand.

"Stop," said Grave. "Is that the gap thing you were talking about?"

"Yes," said Thursday and Blunt in unison. Blunt laughed and motioned Thursday to continue. "Yes, detective, the sequence anomaly."

"And how big was the gap?"

"Let's see." Thursday reversed the tape to the point before the anomaly. "Okay, fourteen minutes after the hour here." She advanced the video and immediately stopped it. "And the time stamp here shows thirty-seven minutes past the hour."

"Twenty-three minutes, sir," said Blunt.

"More than enough time to kill Whitney and pose her on the canvas."

"Got him!" said Blunt.

"So it appears," said Grave. "Okay, Ms. Thursday, let's roll it back to Friday night, say 7:00 pm, so we can see what Smithers was up to before and during the lockdown in the studio."

Thursday hit reverse and the images began to race backwards. Grave grabbed another donut and sipped at his coffee. A solution was at hand—he was sure of it—but he didn't want to rush things, particularly since there were still nine chocolate donuts left.

42

Despite his name, Captain Morgan had no affinity for the sea or sailing at all. His father had cured him of that, taking the young Henry well out into the Chesapeake Bay to fish for bluefish and what his dad called "croakers" and "hardheads." As they fished, or tried to fish—their lines becoming entangled time and time again—a storm came up, the calm waters turning quickly to six-foot swells and Henry just as quickly turning to throw up in the small boat, the former contents of his stomach flowing in waves from port to starboard as the boat rocked and rolled in the swells. He counted it among the worst days of his life, as did his father, who never dared to take Henry fishing again.

The thought of it made him wonder why he had chosen to come to the marina at all instead of just sending an officer, or just calling, but he knew the answer: he was bored out of his skull and thought a brisk walk along the sea would do him good, maybe help him throw off the caloric effects of a chocolate donut or two. To help that idea along, he had parked at the far end of the marina parking lot, so he could walk by all the yachts along the pier on his way to the marina headquarters, home of the yacht club, a low, flat-roofed building with windows all round to afford views of the comings and goings of the wealthy.

The largest yachts, which were more like small passenger liners, bobbed at anchor a hundred yards or so offshore, along with large speedboats that seemed to be racing at high speed even though they were at anchor, their shapes and lines designed to suggest all-out speed.

The racing yachts were tied up in special slips along the pier, each identified by small signs, black letters on white. Captain Morgan tried his best to focus on the signs and not the ships bobbing in the chop created by the strong winds blowing in from the southeast: *Sea Dawg XI, Turner's Tiller, Sail On!, Mosby's Ghost III, My Eleanor, Thorn's Blood, Marvel-At-Us, Whippet Good.*

He stopped and walked back to the sign for *Thorn's Blood*, which was embellished with the image of a golden trophy—the MacGuffin. This was where Hawthorne's yacht belonged, but there was no yacht. The slip was empty.

He picked up his pace and headed for the building, finally pushing through its glass double doors and marching to its reception desk, where a young man caught sight of him and immediately contemplated the advisability of flight, the imposing bulk of a charging Captain Morgan enough to give even the innocent pause.

"May I help you, sir?" the young man stuttered.

Morgan pulled out the business card. "Mr. Thorpe, Grant Horatio Thorpe, if you please."

"Ah, um, well then, I'm afraid Mr. Thorpe is not *here*, sir."

Captain Morgan knew he should have called first, but where's the fun in that. "When do you expect him back?"

Morgan was hoping the young man would say *any minute now,* but instead he said, "Not till tomorrow, I'm afraid."

Morgan sighed in frustration. "Well, you'll have to do, I guess. I'm Captain Morgan, and I'm here to retrieve the MacGuffin Trophy."

The young man chuckled nervously at the name, but quickly recovered. "Oh, well, I'm afraid you're out of luck there as well, captain. Mr. Thorpe took it with him."

"With him?"

"Yes, sir."

"Where?"

The young man shrugged. "I'm not sure, sir, but I know he left with the trophy. Perhaps the insurance company. I know he had been concerned about that ever since the trophy went missing."

This really was annoying. "How long ago?"

The young man checked his watch. "About two hours ago."

"And you're sure he had the trophy?"

"Yes, absolutely. It's hard to miss."

Captain Morgan glowered at the young man, stepped back from the reception desk, and pulled out his cellphone, punching in the number on the business card. The phone rang and rang, but no one answered.

He turned to leave, but then had second thoughts. He went back up to the desk. "A couple of things, young man. If you hear from Mr. Thorpe, please have him call me immediately. It is of the *utmost* importance that we retrieve that trophy."

"Yes, sir, and your number would be . . . ?

Captain Morgan slapped his own business card down on the desk. "Second, can you tell me where Darius Hawthorne's yacht might be?"

The man looked puzzled at first, and then brightened. "Oh, yes, if it's not in its slip, I expect the new owner has it out for a spin."

"New owner?"

"Yes, sir. As I understand it, Mr. Hawthorne sold it just a few days ago."

"Really? Are you sure?" *Why would the winner of the MacGuffin Trophy sell his winning yacht?* And the answer came almost immediately: *He needed money, bad.*

The young man laughed. "Oh, definitely. Mr. Hawthorne was quite animated about it. Came in and told everyone. Made a killing, he said."

"Interesting. A bit odd, don't you think, to sell a winning yacht?"

"Um, I guess." The young man had apparently never given that question a thought. "He *was* excited, though," he added cheerily.

Morgan glowered back. "Well, when the new owner gets back, have *him* give me a call, too."

The young man lowered his voice to a whisper and leaned conspiratorially across the reception desk. "Is this about the *murders,* captain?"

Captain Morgan ignored the question with a dismissive shake of his head, turned, and marched toward the door. Once outside, he instantly regretted parking his car so far away. He trudged on, the smell of the sea and rotting fish keeping him company, the contents of his stomach threatening mutiny.

43

Grave pushed the last bit of his fourth donut into his mouth and watched as Ms. Thursday queued up the video for Friday night, trying his best to ignore the comingled cloud of love that was Sergeant Blunt and Ms. Thursday, who were now Barry and June to each other. Had Grave not been there, he was certain that the studio would be witnessing an uncommon event atop the control panel.

"Here you go," said Thursday. "Time check, 7:03."

Grave, Blunt, and Thursday watched through Smithers' "eyes" as he walked about the vast kitchen, gathering champagne glasses, checking them for spots, and placing them on a large silver tray.

"Stop," said Grave.

The video froze on an image of the tray.

"Twelve glasses," said Grave. "Why so many? Were they expecting more people?"

"Probably allowing for breakage," said Thursday.

"Or maybe the extras are for people who insist on fresh glasses," Blunt cooed back at her.

"Yes, Barry, lipstick and so on," said Thursday, returning the coo.

"Okay," said Grave, hoping they were finished, "we'll make a note of it. Perhaps more people were invited, is all I'm saying. Now, let's fast forward it, but be ready to stop it."

"Yes, sir," said Thursday.

She hit a couple of buttons and Smithers raced around the kitchen, into the foyer, into the elevator, and out of the elevator into the laboratory.

"Slow it down," said Grave.

Thursday dutifully complied, the images slowing to show the line of charging stations, ten of them occupied by simdroids of the Peter O'Toole persuasion. Grave counted to make sure.

"Okay, they're all there," said Grave. "Smithers must have been checking to make sure the charging process was going as expected."

"There he goes again," said Blunt.

Smithers headed back to the elevator, up to the foyer, and back into the kitchen, where he approached a drawer, took out several cloth napkins, put them on the tray, moved to the refrigerator, took out three bottles of champagne, put them on the tray, and started to lift the tray before suddenly stopping, going to a far cupboard, and taking down two ice buckets, which he filled with ice and placed on the tray.

"Ye gods," said Blunt. "Can he really lift all that?"

Thursday laughed. "They're very strong, Barry. This is nothing."

They watched as Smithers lifted the tray and took it up the long flight of stairs and into the studio, placing it on a draped table at the back of the room, just to the side of Whitney's easel. There was no one else in the room.

"Okay, stop it for a second," said Grave.

Thursday complied.

"Now," continued Grave, "let's take it to the point where people start entering the studio. We'll be looking for anything unusual."

"What do you mean, *unusual?*" said Thursday.

"Things that stand out, that aren't quite right," said Blunt.

"Someone doing something out of character, or even little things like what a person brings into the room," said Grave.

"You mean like a person coming in dressed as a cat burglar, carrying a large sack to steal the trophy?"

Grave smiled. "Yes, exactly, but a little more subtle than that. Most importantly, we want to see how people react when it becomes apparent that they are locked in the room. I suspect at least one of them won't be surprised at all."

"Okay," said Thursday. "Shall we begin?"

Grave glanced at the box of donuts, decided he'd had enough for now, and nodded. "Proceed."

The first one in the room was Whitney, who immediately pulled off her clothes, took a glass of champagne from Smithers, and disappeared from view, presumably to stand next to her draped painting of a trophy-like mackerel.

Mr. and Mrs. Hawthorne were next to arrive, both near expressionless, Philomena taking a glass of champagne and Darius waving it off, the MacGuffin Trophy carefully nestled against his chest. Both disappeared from view as the door opened again, the divine Ms. LaFarge wheeling in Edwina Hawthorne, trailed by the Indian chief, Roy Lynn.

"Stop it," said Grave.

The tape came to an abrupt stop, freezing on Edwina's face.

"I have reason to believe that Ms. Hawthorne here can actually move her body, so pay particular attention to her every time she comes into view. The position of her hands and so on. Ms. Thursday, if you see anything at all, stop the tape on your own. That goes for you, too, Blunt. If you see something, shout out."

Thursday pressed go and the tape resumed, Smithers walking around the room with a tray of filled champagne glasses as the guests milled about, waiting for the grand unveiling. Grave watched with interest as Ms. LaFarge worked her way through glass after glass of champagne, accepting each one as Smithers made his rounds. Edwina sat in place not far from the door.

Young Roy Lynn seemed to appear in almost every frame, arrows whizzing in all directions, one even taking out a glass of champagne on Smithers' tray, the glass exploding, Thursday gasping in surprise.

She suddenly stopped the video. "Look, there behind the glasses. The naked woman there."

"Whitney Waters," said Blunt.

"Whomever," said Thursday. "She looks angry. Who's she talking to?"

Grave leaned in. "That's her parents, the Hawthornes. Can you make out what they're saying?"

"Sorry, detective, I don't read lips."

"Why don't we have audio?" said Blunt.

"His series records video by default, sound only by request," said

Thursday.

"Odd, don't you think?" said Grave "Anyway, our CSI folks might be able to parse that out. Make a note of the time stamp, and let's start it up again."

The video resumed, Smithers' tray moving on, leaving the brief argument behind. Ms. LaFarge took another glass of champagne, and Smithers wheeled back toward the door, where Whitney was tugging at the doorknob. And then he was turning back toward Mr. and Mrs. Hawthorne, who were standing next to the easel, Philomena checking her watch and Darius staring blankly into space. The MacGuffin trophy sat on a small table in front of the easel, perhaps so people could wonder at and compare the real thing against Whitney's red mackerel interpretation.

Smithers suddenly wheeled his tray around. Whitney was tugging at the doorknob, struggling to open the door and shouting something over her shoulder. An arrow whizzed by her head. Ms. LaFarge appeared, also trying the door. Then Smithers set down the tray and tried to open the door without success. Whitney appeared in the frame again, raising her hands in frustration, and shouting angrily toward the back of the room.

Smithers then turned back and walked toward the easel. Darius and Philomena had not moved.

"Stop," shouted Grave. The image froze on Darius, Philomena, the still-draped easel, and the small table in front of it.

"What?" said Thursday.

"The table," said Grave. "No MacGuffin."

Blunt whistled through his teeth. "It's gone."

"Like magic," said Thursday.

"Indeed," said Grave. "Roll it back, and let's have a second look."

A second look became a third look, and a fourth, but the MacGuffin Trophy mysteriously disappeared each time. They rolled it back a fifth time, measuring the time between Ms. LaFarge's appearance at the door and Smithers' turn to show the Hawthornes and the empty table.

"I get twelve seconds," said Blunt. "More than enough time to hide the trophy."

"But where?" said Grave. "And where's Edwina and Roy Lynn

when all of this was going on?"

They rolled it back a sixth time, this time to judge the trajectory of the whizzing arrows.

"I'm thinking Roy Lynn's shooting from somewhere to the side of the easel," said Grave, "but halfway to the door. Not much of an arc in the trajectory, which suggests a fairly close shot."

"I agree, sir," said Blunt, "but where is Edwina?"

"Good point," said Grave. "Ms. Thursday, roll it back until we see her, then roll it forward until we see her again."

"No problem," said Thursday.

She rolled it back. Edwina was sitting in her wheelchair, Ms. LaFarge standing next to her. Thursday advanced the tape through the door-tugging scene. No Edwina. She rolled it further along.

"There," shouted Blunt.

Edwina was still in her wheelchair, but she was no longer along the wall near the front of the room. She was at the very back of the room, behind the easel and to the left, which would have given her a clear view of everyone—and everything that had happened.

"How did she get there?" said Blunt.

"It's not clear from the tape," said Grave. "I suppose it's possible that Roy Lynn pushed her along between arrows, but I think not."

"Well, somebody moved her," said Blunt.

Thursday brightened. "What about the Hawthornes? They could have done it, too. And Whitney had disappeared briefly."

"And Edwina would have been the perfect foil to act as cart for the trophy," said Blunt, "considering her physical and mental state."

"Yes, but more to the point," said Grave, "why bring the trophy *into* the room just to mysteriously steal it away?"

"A distraction of some kind?" offered Thursday.

"There's certainly that, and then there's the real conundrum," said Blunt. "How could they have killed Ms. Jones?"

"We're back to the locked room again," said Grave.

"Or more than one murderer," said Blunt.

They sat there in silence, each trying to make sense of what they knew and what they had seen on the videos, Blunt and Thursday not exactly pulling their weight, their eyes locked on each other.

Grave broke the silence. "All that aside, it looks like we have a witness. Perhaps she can help us unlock the rest."

Blunt shook his head. "But how is she really a witness? I mean, she can't even talk—or communicate."

Grave smiled up at him. "You never know, Blunt."

Thursday was mystified. "Why the British accent, detective?"

44

Reviewing the remaining tapes had taken them well into the evening and was revealing only to the extent that it revealed nothing, at least from the other ten robots. What it did reveal was that there must have been another robot, the one the murderer had used to retrieve the hand from the morgue.

Polk had called in late afternoon to let Grave know that the blood collected from the Smithers simcortex had matched the blood type for Whitney Hawthorne, as well as for Epiphany Jones. They'd have to wait for additional test results to determine whether the blood belonged to Whitney, Epiphany, or both.

Grave knew that additional interviews would be needed to lock down the case, particularly with Edwina, but he was now certain, at least in his gut, that Darius Hawthorne had murdered Whitney, perhaps with the help of his wife, Philomena. He suspected their involvement in the murder of Epiphany Jones as well, given the method of death, but the puzzle piece that would complete the puzzle remained as elusive as the MacGuffin Trophy and its role in the murders, if any.

Captain Morgan had called as Grave was trying to wrap things up and coax a reluctant Sergeant Blunt into the Sprite. The man just didn't want to take a single step away from his new love, June Thursday.

The captain related his unfruitful excursion to the marina to retrieve the trophy, which was now "somewhere with this Thorpe fellow."

Grave filled him in on what they had found on the videos, and Morgan had reluctantly agreed with Grave's understanding of the facts. Morgan would work on an arrest warrant for the Hawthornes, which he proposed acting on at the conclusion of the funeral. Grave thought that would be overly dramatic, and pushed for an immediate arrest, but Morgan was having none of it.

"If we did that, the mayor would be all over me. Let them have their goddamn funeral."

Grave had just sighed heavily into the cellphone.

"Look, if you're right," said Morgan, "a few hours won't make a bit of difference."

"Can we at least double the number of officers at the mansion? I don't want them fleeing."

Morgan had agreed and terminated the conversation without so much as a goodbye.

Grave finally tore Blunt and Thursday apart, near dragging him into the Sprite, and drove him back to the precinct so he could pick up his own car and drive home. Ms. Thursday, bless her, had agreed to take the simcortexes back to the mansion, so the simdroids could resume their duties. Grave fully expected her to hook up with Blunt later that evening, two clouds on the town with a third cloud: cloud nine.

45

Grave woke up the next morning fully expecting to hear the sound of rain, but apparently the elements had conspired to avoid funeral clichés and had pushed out a bright, sunny day, one more appropriate for picnics and sailing, not that he had done either in quite some time, given the number of women and sailing boats in his life, which upon reflection was zero, and upon further reflection remained zero. He had high hopes for Ms. LaFarge, but that would have to wait until the dust settled on this case, if it happened at all. He was one of those men who didn't know how to make the pitch, let alone close the sale, so anything resembling a relationship was elusive.

He hurriedly dressed, selecting one of his many gray suits and fumbling through the closet for a gray or black tie, ending up with a gray tie with black polka dots, a tie he had bought for a fancy cocktail party that had not gone well. It would just have to do. He found his dress shoes, dusted them off, and managed to squeeze his feet in. They pinched at the toes, but he only had to wear them for a couple of hours, so he kept them on rather than reverting to his usual black walking shoes. He felt he needed something else, a black armband or something—anything that would indicate respect for the dead, but armbands were something his closet couldn't come up with, so he opted instead for a black fedora, a narrow-brimmed Dobbs given to him by his father years ago to acknowledge his first collar.

Suitably attired, he had a quick meal of burnt toast and coffee, and headed out the door to the waiting Sprite. He started up the engine, and the gospel choir sprang to life in mid-song, extolling the virtues of the virtuous life and the wondrous afterlife with the Lord.

Ten minutes later, at exactly 44:37 according to his watch, and without a single word from Reverend Bendigo Bottoms, Grave pulled the car into the cemetery and drove along ever-narrowing lanes to the gravesite, where he could see a small somber group of people in black standing in front of a gleaming red coffin, which was being lowered into the ground. He was late!

Everyone turned and looked at him and the car with the full-throated gospel choir as if he were arriving in a chariot pulled by angels. He hurriedly parked and turned off the engine, the last strains of the choir seeming to evaporate on the wind. Captain Morgan, standing at the back of the mourners, along with what must have been Sergeant Blunt and Ms. Thursday, two dark clouds on the fringes, waved for him to hurry up.

Walking fast while appearing to be in somber mourning is not an art form many people practice, and neither had Grave, so it was fortunate that the mourners were watching the casket being lowered into the ground instead of him, because what they would have seen was a man speed-walking like a penguin and occasionally stumbling on grave markers and small clusters of faux flowers.

He walked up beside Captain Morgan and whispered as whispery as he could. "Sorry, sir."

Captain Morgan said nothing, but opened the side of his coat to reveal the arrest warrants, and then turned back to watch the ceremony, which was drawing to a close, everyone's head bowed for a closing prayer.

Mr. and Mrs. Hawthorne sat on small folding chairs at the front, both looking down, Edwina beside them in her wheelchair. Ms. LaFarge, who looked spectacular in black, was standing to the side, holding hands with Darth Vader, who held his light saber out by way of a final salute. Smithers and the other robots stood to the side in a perfect line, as if they were about to issue a twenty-one gun salute, albeit without the involvement of guns or an additional ten robots.

The minister, a tall gaunt man in black, with perhaps three remaining gray hairs on his head, snapped his bible closed with the authority of the Lord and offered a final amen, the signal for all to disperse. Ms. LaFarge was the first to move, bending over to scoop up a little dirt and sprinkle it on the top of the coffin. Darth Vader thought that was a good idea, too, but decided to kick the dirt in, which Ms. LaFarge put a stop to immediately, yanking him back and whispering loudly in his ear to "fuckin' stop."

Darth relented and walked along beside her as Ms. LaFarge pushed Edwina toward the waiting handicap van, trailed by Smithers and the other robots.

She spotted Grave and gave him a warm smile. "So good of you to come, detective." Then she had managed a small laugh. "Nice hat."

Grave nodded, thinking to say something, but came up with nothing, letting her pass right by him, along with Darth and Edwina, who seemed to have tears in her eyes. Grave couldn't wait to interview her again.

The Hawthornes, who would be the last to leave, remained seated in front of the open grave, heads down, unmoving, as if locked in unbearable grief. The minister glanced at his watch and walked away, leaving them there to share a final moment with their daughter, as a backhoe rumbled to life, the cemetery staff eager to complete the process and move on to the next gravesite.

Grave turned to Captain Morgan, who nodded and pulled the arrest warrants from his suit, handing them to Grave. The four of them approached the Hawthornes, Ms. Thursday hanging back, not wanting to intrude on an official arrest.

Grave moved around the Hawthornes and took the position vacated by the minister. "Darius and Philomena Hawthorne," he said, "you are under arrest for the murders of Ms. Epiphany Jones and your daughter, Whitney Waters." He continued on, issuing the full Miranda warning, advising them of their rights.

The Hawthornes just sat there, unmoving.

Captain Morgan and Blunt came up beside them as Grave tried again to break them from their paralysis of grief.

"Darius, Philomena, I'm afraid you'll have to come with us now." He placed his hand on Darius Hawthorne's shoulder, but the man did not respond.

Ms. Thursday let out a little gasp and rushed up to Grave, pointing at the backs of the Hawthornes, where the thin handles of simcortexes protruded.

"These turkeys are done," she said.

"Two more murders?" shouted Captain Morgan, incredulous.

"No, sir," said Thursday. "Just two simdroids who've lost their charge."

Grave stood there, mouth agape, dumbstruck.

46

To say that Grave had gravely misunderstood the facts was perhaps the understatement of the year, at least at the precinct, where the snickering had already begun. Every time Grave glanced outside the fishbowl, he thought he saw yet another officer laughing at him. It was humiliating.

"Grave, wake up," said Captain Morgan. "We need to sort this out."

Grave nodded and glanced left and right, where Blunt and Thursday sat, giving him encouraging looks.

"Yes, sir." He really didn't know what to say.

Fortunately, the phone rang, giving him more time to figure out how to proceed.

Captain Morgan picked up the phone, said hello, then quickly covered the phone with his hand. "It's that marina guy, you know, Thorpe, the MacGuffin thingy."

"Yes, sir," said Captain Morgan, "I've been meaning to talk to you about that trophy. We really—"

A look of disbelief came over the captain's face, his mouth dropping open. "I see, I see. Well, then, I'll get back to you. Yes, yes, of course we'll take this seriously. Goodbye."

Morgan slumped back in his chair, the others looking at him expectantly. "Seems the MacGuffin Trophy is not the *real* MacGuffin Trophy."

"What?" said Grave, sitting bolt upright.

"He just got back from the insurance company. Apparently, it's a fake, ginned up with a 3-D printer, they think."

Bells, whistles, and skyrockets were going off in Grave's mind, puzzle pieces spinning, locking into place. "Of course, of course!" he shouted.

"What?" said Captain Morgan.

"They're stealing the MacGuffin!"

"The Hawthornes?"

"Yes!"

Morgan leapt to his feet. "Blunt, get on the horn. We need to close the airport and the train station."

"No, wait, captain," said Grave. "I think they'll be taking their yacht."

"But he sold it," said Morgan. "No, wait, it was not in its slip yesterday. Do you think?"

"Yes, there was no sale at all. Just a ruse to throw us off the track." He suddenly remembered the travel brochures at Epiphany's apartment. "In fact, I think if you google Iceland, Cuba, Bolivia, Ecuador, and Nicaragua, you'll find that they have one thing in common—no extradition treaty with the United States."

"They're making a run for it, heading for safe harbors," said Thursday.

"But which?" said Blunt.

"It really doesn't matter," said Grave. "They've got a head start on us, but not enough to reach any of those destinations. Blunt, get on the phone to the Coast Guard. They'll have to look north and south."

Captain Morgan picked up his phone. "I'll call the marina. They should have a photograph of the boat we can wire to the Coast Guard, and perhaps they can tell us just how fast that yacht sails. Let's get those sons of bitches!"

The officers outside the fishbowl knew that something had changed dramatically, which was usually the case when Captain Morgan made a call while standing, eyes bugged out, face glowing red. They just hoped it wouldn't involve them.

47

The Coast Guard found and boarded the *Thorn's Blood* within hours, taking into custody the Hawthornes, a combative simdroid bearing a striking resemblance to Peter O'Toole, and another simdroid resembling no actor at all, along with the MacGuffin Trophy. An unidentified man in scuba gear had eluded capture by jumping overboard as the Coast Guard vessel approached, and was officially listed as missing at sea.

"Who was that, do you think?" said Captain Morgan, munching on a victory donut.

"I think we'll find it was none other than Chester Clink," said Grave.

"Holy crap!" said Morgan. "We almost had him?"

Ms. Thursday cleared her throat. "You mean that serial killer?"

"Yes," said Blunt. "Philomena's brother."

"Whoa," said Thursday. "Curiouser and curiouser."

"Indeed," said Grave.

"I must admit," said Thursday, "having come into the middle of all this, I haven't a clue how everything fits together. Why two murders?"

Grave stood and paced the room as he spoke, the only way he knew to work through the puzzle. The motive for the first murder had been greed. Darius Hawthorne needed money, and with the art market in the tank, so had Epiphany Jones. She and Darius had come up with a scheme to sell the MacGuffin Trophy to a foreign collector.

It had been a reasonable plan. Darius would build robot clones of himself and Philomena, as well as a new simdroid with a killing protocol to help them in their escape, if necessary.

Thursday gasped. "That's unheard of—and scary!"

"Yes," said Grave, "and that's not the half of it."

He resumed his explication. The plan had been to create a replica of the trophy, with the real trophy stored in Epiphany's safe until the time they would make their escape. The replica, of course, would be "stolen," hopefully throwing off the police as the Hawthornes and Epiphany made their escape.

"So that's why they left the phony in the safe, so we'd think we'd solved the case," said Blunt. "But something went wrong with the plan. More greed, I suspect."

"Yes," said Grave. "On the night of her murder, she was to bring the real MacGuffin to the mansion, but she didn't. She wanted a bigger share of the profits, and Hawthorne was having none of it."

"Bingo bango, she's killed," said Captain Morgan.

"By Hawthorne?" said Thursday.

"It's possible, certainly," said Grave, "but I think when we get them back here for interrogation, we'll find it was Chester Clink himself or a simdroid built to resemble him."

Captain Morgan seemed startled. "I don't follow."

Grave continued his pacing and parsing, laying out his understanding of the facts. Clink's last two murders had involved a different signature, the placement of a single rose in the mouth of the victim. Changing a long-held pattern after so many successful killings would not have been something Clink would have done. He loved the attention too much. But it would be something he and Hawthorne could direct a simdroid to do.

"I still don't get it," said Captain Morgan. "Why go to the trouble?"

"I'm not sure," said Grave. "It could have been an experiment, a way to test the capabilities of a new—and lethal—generation of simdroids. Or maybe Clink saw this as a way to retire but still keep his hand in the game. Perhaps Darius will be able to shed some light on this. In any case, Ms. Jones arrives, makes her demands, and is killed outright, her body dragged through the laboratory, into the elevator, and up to the foyer, where her body is displayed using the new Clink signature rose, torn hastily from the mansion's gardens, along with the arrow and the happy face to further confuse the situation—yet another way to divert attention away from the robbery. And for whatever reason, they inadvertently left the severed hand behind, the hand they knew they would need to unlock Epiphany's safe."

"And all the while, everyone else is upstairs in the studio?" said Thursday.

Grave nodded and continued, moving on to the locked room. The Hawthornes wanted witnesses to the disappearance of the trophy, witnesses who would also vouch for them and throw the police further off the track, the locked room providing a perfect alibi for all of them.

"Okay," said Blunt. "So if the real Hawthorne was in the lab, then his look-alike simdroid would have been in the studio."

"With the simdroid for Philomena?" said Thursday.

"Yes and no," said Grave. "Hawthorne's simdroid was there with the real Philomena. The woman I met in that studio was not the same woman I interviewed. I knew there was something off about her, and there was, because I was interviewing her robotic clone."

Thursday suddenly brightened. "Got it!"

"Got what?" said Blunt.

"How they did it," said Thursday. She turned to Grave. "You're probably well ahead of me, detective, but what must have happened is that while everyone else was distracted by the locked door, Philomena had taken the replica trophy and stashed it in the back of the Hawthorne simdroid."

"Have you ever considered a career in law enforcement?" said Grave, "because you're spot on. She did exactly that, and walked out of the room the next morning, whereupon the real Mr. Hawthorne took the replica back to Ephiphany's apartment, exchanged it for the real trophy, and brought it back to the mansion."

"And then they made their escape," said Captain Morgan.

"Leaving the fake Mr. and Mrs. Hawthorne behind, to throw us off the scent," said Blunt.

"Yes," said Grave, "and that led to the unfortunate—and wholly unplanned—murder of Whitney."

"But why?" said Thursday.

"Remember, Whitney was in quite a state, lashing out at anything and anyone. The Hawthorne simdroid happened to be on the receiving end of a heavy blow that cut through its fake skin."

"Of course," said Thursday. "That explains the surprised look on her face. She would have seen the robotic internals of the simdroid."

"So the simdroid pulled the simcortex out of Smithers, simultaneously eliminating the only witness while providing itself with a murder weapon."

"Exactly," said Grave.

He sat back down and closed his eyes, reflecting on everything that had transpired. "Yes," he said, opening his eyes and looking at each of them in turn. "Yes, yes, yes, that is *exactly* how it was done.

They sat there in silence for some moments, each reflecting on what had transpired.

Thursday was the first to speak. "I don't get it."

"What?" said Grave.

"It seems so complex. I mean, why go to all that trouble? Why not just grab the trophy, jump on the yacht, and sail away?"

"It certainly would have been the simplest solution," said Blunt. "You know, Occam's razor and all that."

Thursday seemed puzzled. "I'm sorry, what?"

"Occam's razor," said Grave, "a philosophical idea that suggests that the simplest answer to a problem is the most probable answer."

"Well, Grave, you have to admit she has a point," said Captain Morgan. "Custom robots, a fake trophy, a freakin' locked room. Come on."

"The thing is," said Grave, "it's never a case of pure logic. It's always the perpetrator's logic we're dealing with, and that is more likely than not a twisted, hall-of-mirrors reflection of the criminal's personality and motivation. Hawthorne had been fired by the company he had started. What better way to stick it to them than to develop custom robots far beyond the capabilities of Ramrod robots."

"And the locked room?" said Thursday.

"Just part of an intricate puzzle, as was the fake trophy," said Grave. "Another way to express his superior intelligence."

"Or so he thought," said Blunt.

"Yes," said Grave. "And his mistake was a simple one, trusting Ms. Jones, who was greedier than he had imagined."

"So it all unraveled," said Captain Morgan.

"But first it became more complicated," said Grave, "moving farther and farther away from Occam's razor. It's like my father always says: the more people involved in a crime, the less likely its success."

Captain Morgan started to say something about Grave's father, but thought better of it. He glanced at his watch. "It's 27:53," he said. "Let's wrap this up."

48

The Hawthornes would not arrive back at the precinct until the next morning, so Captain Morgan had given them leave to take the rest of the day off. Grave's toast and coffee had worn off completely, so on the spur of the moment, he had diverted the Sprite and its gospel choir down Main Street, to the Skunk 'n Donuts a few doors down from Epiphany's apartment. The crime scene tape was still there, rippling in the breeze.

Grave whipped into a parking space, fed the meter, and walked into the donut shop, which was filled with donuts of every kind, including chocolate donuts, but not many customers—a young couple giggling at a table in the corner, and an older man dressed all in black, sipping at his coffee at a table near the window.

The teenager behind the counter seemed to be a clone of the teenager he had encountered at the other Skunk 'n Donuts, and just as quick to talk to him.

"What'll it be, sir?"

"Coffee and a chocolate donut. No, make that *two* chocolate donuts."

The kid smiled back at him and scurried away to fill the order. A voice—a familiar voice coming from the man near the window—startled Grave.

He spun around. The man was talking into a small recording device, his voice rich and deep.

"And so sayeth the Lord," the man said, clicking off the recorder.

Grave walked over to the man's table. "You're Reverend Bendigo Bottoms, aren't you?"

The man looked up and smiled. "The one and only."

Grave smiled back at him. "I'm a big fan."

"Really?" said the reverend. "I don't get that from many white folks."

"Their loss."

"Indeed." The reverend stared up at Grave, expecting him to say more, but Grave just stood there staring down at him.

"Um, is there something I can help you with, my son?"

Grave smiled down at him again. "Yes, I think there is."

"Well, out with it, then."

"I have a question, something that's been bothering me the last couple of days."

"Ask and ye shall receive, brother."

"Okay," said Grave, taking a deep breath. "How *is* life like a tuna fish sandwich?"

The reverend chuckled. "Ah, have a seat, my son. We have much to discuss."

Epilogue

The weeks that followed had been a whirlwind for Detective Simon Grave. Darius Hawthorne had confirmed Grave's understanding of the facts, and had been distraught about his daughter's death, a reaction not shared by Philomena, who remained silent, refusing to talk even to her lawyer. Both were quickly charged.

The four evil simdroids, including the custom droids for Chester, Darius, and Philomena, were safely locked away in the evidence room, awaiting their use in the upcoming trial. The good simdroids, including Smithers, continued on at the mansion, going about their business in their typical, emotionally detached way.

Chester Clink remained at large and possibly still at sea. The Coast Guard continued its search, but Grave suspected Clink had escaped their grasp once again.

The Yacht Club had clearly learned a valuable lesson, and was quick to take advantage of an "extra" trophy, the priceless MacGuffin locked away at a secret location protected by a laser light show, the faux trophy becoming the one loaned to the winner of the annual race.

If there was a silver lining in murder, its recipients had been Calamity Jones and Roy Lynn Waters, and to a lesser extent, Jeremy Polk. Cal had taken ownership of the gallery and was making a killing collecting commissions on the renewed interest in Whitney's remaining paintings. The bulk of those revenues were going to Roy Lynn, of course. Even the scraps of the paintings involved with her death were selling well, a two-inch square scrap selling for over a thousand dollars. The big haul, of course, was from the painting now called "Still Death with Artist," which went at auction for over seventy-five million dollars, to an unknown Japanese collector. Darth Vader was set for life, and could probably afford to build a Death Star.

Jeremy Polk, who had the odd foresight to purchase several of Whitney's red herring, or rather red mackerel, paintings, earned enough money through the sale of just one painting to buy a Lamborghini, which he insisted on flaunting every time he encountered Simon and his diminutive Sprite.

Darth's aunt, Edwina, had made a full recovery and was granted custody of Roy Lynn. Her recovery was particularly pleasing to Grave, who had been instrumental in bringing her back to life. He had only to wheel her into a room and force her to watch episode after episode of Masterpiece Theater. By the end of the first episode, her fingers and eyes were twitching. By the end of the fourth, she was able to stand and walk around. By the end of the sixth, she was able to speak again, rattling on nonstop about the murders and what she had seen. Most significant was why she had gone catatonic in the first place. She had witnessed her mother's killing, at the hands of then Philomena Clink, who had pushed her mother off the catwalk above the plant floor of Ramrod Robotics, her first step toward marrying Darius Hawthorne.

As all of this was going on, Sergeant Blunt and Ms. Thursday continued courting, leading to a quick engagement, the date set for just a month later, in the place where they had first met, the lobby of Ramrod Robotics.

The last piece of the puzzle fell into place two weeks later, with the unexpected arrival of the divine Ms. LaFarge on Simon Grave's doorstep, a bottle of wine in her hands.

"How did you find me?" Grave said.

"Detective, it's not that hard."

Grave glanced down at the wine. "Would you like to come in?"

"No, I'm just delivering wine."

"Oh."

"No, silly, of course I want to come in."

She pushed past him and headed for the kitchen, Grave admiring her as he walked along behind her.

"You're not one to make the first move, are you, detective?

"I guess not."

"It's been *weeks*, you know. No warrants, no subpoenas, not even a phone call."

"Um."

She started opening kitchen cupboards. "Where are the glasses? *Men*, I swear you have no sense of order."

"Next one over," said Grave.

She pulled down two wine glasses, checked them for spots, and began unscrewing the top to the wine.

"It's called Duct Tape Chardonnay," she said. "The wine that can fix anything."

"Oh," said Grave, "do you think I need fixing?"

She raised her eyebrows and giggled. "Oh, yes."

"Really?"

She walked over and grabbed him by his tie. "Shall we start with logic?"

If she had let him speak, he would have said that a detective's job is as much about *revealing* logic as it is about using logic. But as illogical as it seems, she just reeled him in and kissed him, a kiss so disarming he decided he would have to discuss it with Master Cho and his fellow Hap Wadoo warriors.

Needless to say, the evening had gone far better than Grave could ever have imagined. It was the kind of evening that some might describe in explicit terms involving glistening, intertwined bodies and personal hydraulics, but Grave was old school, preferring more tasteful descriptions featuring crashing waves, exploding fireworks, and rockets blasting off into space.

In the end—and let there be no misunderstanding—he could only agree that life was indeed like a tuna fish sandwich.

Other books by Len Boswell:

Simon Grave Series:
Simon Grave and the Curious Incident
of the Cat in the Daytime

Flicker: A Paranormal Mystery

Skeleton: A Bare Bones Mystery

The Leadership Secrets of Squirrels

Santa Takes a Tumble

Thank you so much for reading one of our **Mystery-Thriller** novels.
If you enjoyed our book, please check out our recommended title for your
next great read!

The sequel to *A Grave Misunderstanding* by Len Boswell

Simon Grave and the Curious Incident of the Cat in the Daytime
(release date February 28, 2019)

"Boswell continues his genre-defying series in this
ambitious adventure..." **—Publishers Weekly**

"It is a rare experience to be in suspense about what will happen next even
as I am laughing out loud." **—Michael Hartnett, Fools in the Magic Kingdom**

"Another hysterical whodunit. The cat's meow!"
—Courtney Filigenzi, Clover Doves

View other Black Rose Writing titles at www.blackrosewriting.com/books

and use promo code **PRINT** to receive a **20% discount** when purchasing

CPSIA information can be obtained
at www.ICGtesting.com
Printed in the USA
LVHW041453160419
614374LV00001B/231/P